GOING, GOING, GONE

IN DUE TIME

GOING, GOING, GONE
by Nicholas O. Time

SIMON SPOTLIGHT

New York   London   Toronto   Sydney   New Delhi

Special thanks to the Reference Library at the National Baseball Hall of Fame and Museum for their help.

Great souls are great inspirers. —L. G. Akita
For Felipe, master inspirer and best coach ever, with love —S. S. H.

SIMON SPOTLIGHT
An imprint of Simon & Schuster Children's Publishing Division
1230 Avenue of the Americas, New York, New York 10020
This Simon Spotlight hardcover edition July 2016
Copyright © 2016 by Simon & Schuster, Inc.
Text by Sheila Sweeny Higginson. Cover illustration by Stephen Gilpin.
All rights reserved, including the right of reproduction in whole or in part in any form. SIMON SPOTLIGHT and colophon are registered trademarks of Simon & Schuster, Inc. For information about special discounts for bulk purchases, please contact Simon & Schuster Special Sales at 1-866-506-1949 or business@simonandschuster.com.
Designed by Jay Colvin. The text of this book was set in Adobe Garamond Pro.
Manufactured in the United States of America 0516 FFG
10 9 8 7 6 5 4 3 2 1
ISBN 978-1-4814-6730-8 (hc)
ISBN 978-1-4814-6729-2 (pbk)
ISBN 978-1-4814-6731-5 (eBook)
Library of Congress Control Number 2016936490

Time moves in one direction,
memory in another.
—William Gibson

Your shoulder's open," Grandpa Joe says for the 47,718th time of my twelve-year-long life. "Check yourself."

I sigh deeply into my glove so my grandfather won't hear me. It's annoying listening to those exact words *every single time* I practice with him. It's even more annoying knowing that he's usually right. Well, to be honest, more like *always* right.

Grandpa Joe lobs the ball back to me. I carefully move my fingers around the seams to get the right grip. I try to stop thinking about how annoyed I feel, and set my mind on my balance instead.

"Check your feet, kiddo," Grandpa reminds me, pointing down at my sneakers.

Oh yeah, my feet. I set them into the position Grandpa taught me when I was barely big enough to hold a ball in my hand. I bend my knees so I'm loose, then I take a deep breath. Eyes focused on my target, I pull back into my balance point, hold my shoulder in line with my eyes, shift to power position, and throw the ball as hard as I can. It hits Grandpa's glove dead in the center with a loud *thwack!*

"There you go!" Grandpa cheers. "Who's on your side, Matt?"

"You are, Grandpa," I reply for the 47,718th time. "Always."

I hear the familiar sound of rugged tires crunching the gravel in our driveway. Have I mentioned that it's only 7:30 a.m.? And that I've been throwing a baseball for thirty minutes already? And that I still have a full day of school— and a play-off game—ahead of me? Welcome to the world of Matt Vezza. It's an exhausting place!

My best friend, Luis Ramirez, is sitting on his dirt bike, waiting for me to grab my stuff so we can ride to school together. He looks at me, grins, and shakes his head.

"Okay, I know you're a pretty good pitcher, but are you *ever* going to learn how to throw a baseball like your grandpa, dude?" Luis chuckles as he tips his bucket hat at my grandfather. "Morning, Grandpa Joe."

"Morning, Luis," Grandpa Joe replies.

Grandpa Joe tosses the ball to Luis. I put my head down and pretend to stare at the ground, because I know what's sure to come next when Luis tosses the ball back. Shoulder open, grip totally wrong, the ball flies wildly up over Grandpa Joe's head. He reaches up and grabs it like the pro ballplayer that he almost was, but I can see the pain flash through his face when he reaches down and rubs his ankle.

"Are you okay, Grandpa?" I say, trying to sound nonchalant, but concerned. I know Grandpa Joe's pain has been getting worse and worse, even though he's been trying to hide it.

"Okay? I've got more energy than you two combined!" Grandpa Joe says proudly. "And if *you* ever want to learn to throw a baseball, I'll be here waiting, Luis."

"Thanks, Grandpa Joe, but you know baseball's not my thing," Luis says with a laugh. He twirls his bucket hat on his finger for a moment and then tosses it in the air. It lands perfectly on his head. Even I have to admit, it's pretty impressive.

I give Grandpa a quick pat good-bye on the back, then hop on my bike. I know he loves me, but Grandpa isn't exactly the hugging type. He's old school in every way. I just wish I got a chance to see him when he was young.

"Grandpa Joe is mad cool," Luis yells to me. "But baseball? Dude, it is sooooo boring."

"It's only boring if you don't understand the game," I say, sounding like a Grandpa Joe clone. Sometimes I can't help myself. It's scary.

We ride up Park Street, make a left on Pine, and then hit Washington Avenue. Sands Middle School is standing proudly in the distance, eagerly awaiting our arrival.

"Hey, Matt, are you ready for . . . ," Luis calls as we race toward the bike rack. Then he makes a cone with his hands and shouts through it, "TRRRREEEMMMMT TIME?"

Luis is referring to Ms. Tremt, our school librarian. It's Wednesday, so we have library first period.

Ms. Tremt seems all right to me, but she's always been the subject of cafeteria gossip. It might be the furry, incredibly colorful scarves she likes to wear, even when it's eighty degrees outside. Or the boxes and boxes of library books that never seem to disappear, no matter how much unpacking we do for her. But most likely, it's the way she sits silently and stares at one student for nearly the entire period while we're reading. Which could seem totally creepy, except that after she stares at you for a while, Ms. Tremt always comes over and hands you a book that you fall in love with from the first paragraph, or the perfect book to help with your science report. It's like she's psychic or something.

"I'm actually looking forward to library today," I tell Luis.

"Oh no!" Luis gasps. "It's finally happened. My best friend has been invaded by AN ALIEN BODY SNATCHER!"

Luis grabs his throat and pretends like he's gasping for air. Then he tumbles to the floor.

"Always a comedian." I laugh. "I'm serious, though. Ms. Tremt said she was going to order me a book about New York baseball in 1951. I want to see if it came in yet. I never mentioned anything to her about 1951. Or New York. I just told her I'd like to read any books she had about baseball history and she chose that specific year and place. Weird."

"You and baseball." Luis sighs. "So much love. I just don't get it. And who cares about games played sixty years ago?"

I wait a second. Then I can practically see the lightbulb go off over Luis's head.

"Ohhhh . . . 1951 . . . *New York* baseball," he says. "Wasn't Grandpa Joe supposed to play for the Giants that year? Now I get it."

"Yup. 1951 . . . It was a great time to be a baseball fan in New York," I say. "You had three home teams to choose from—the New York

Yankees, the New York Giants, or the Brooklyn Dodgers. And if you think the rivalry between the New York Mets and New York Yankees is fierce today, you should read about the rivalries back then! If you lived in Brooklyn, there was no way you could be a Yankees or Giants fan. You were a Dodgers fan all the way."

"And I'm guessing you want to learn more about what baseball was like in the time when Grandpa Joe almost made the major leagues?" Luis says.

"It takes you a while, but you're not nearly as clueless as you look," I say with a chuckle.

"Hey, leave the jokes to the professional," a voice says from behind me.

I turn around and see Grace Scott standing there, balancing a huge wobbly pile of books in her hands.

"I believe by professional, you are referring to me? Funny friend, at your service," Luis teases. "Just a little light reading, huh, Gracie?"

"A little," Grace replies. "I wanted to get Ms. Tremt's opinion on some of my favorite books. She always has great suggestions about what type of books I should be reading."

"Ms. Tremt wants our minds . . . and our *sooouls*," Luis says, doing the dramatic thing with his hand and voice again. "That's why she stares so deeply at us."

Luis is interrupted by the sound of the first bell. Sands Middle School is open for business. I grab a stack of Grace's books and hand them to Luis, then take a stack myself. We all know the pile will be scattered across the hallowed halls of our school if we leave them in Grace's hands. She's . . . um . . . how shall I put this? Working on improving her balancing skills at the moment. Actually, more like for the past twelve years.

(Don't ever tell Grace I told you this, but in second grade, a couple of mean kids started calling her "Grace-less" behind her back. Luis and I put a stop to that—real fast. We may seem like an odd bunch of bananas, as my grandpa would say, but a friend is a friend. And *nobody* messes with one of our friends.)

After a quick homeroom check-in, we race down the hall and stagger into the library twelve seconds before the first-period bell rings.

Ms. Tremt's scarf is particularly furry today and a shade of green that I have never seen before in my life. It looks almost like a caterpillar . . . a vibrating, furry caterpillar . . . a vibrating, furry, *hungry* caterpillar, just like the one in my favorite book when I was a little . . . Wait, what? Is Ms. Tremt's scarf hypnotizing me or something? That's so weird.

"Matthew," Ms. Tremt says, smiling as she hands me a book. "I believe you were waiting for this?"

"Huh?" I say, still wondering where the whole caterpillar trail of thought came from.

Then I take a look at the book. *It Was the Shot Heard 'Round the World: The Amazing Story of the 1951 Giants-Dodgers Pennant Race.* Perfect!

"Thanks, Ms. Tremt!" I say. "I *was* waiting for this. I was really looking forward to library today."

"Just in the nick of time," Ms. Tremt chirps. "I've been meaning to brush up on my baseball trivia. I can't wait to hear what happens when you turn back the hands of the clock and dig into this one."

I take the book over to a table where Luis and Grace are already sitting. We open our books and start to read. Luis is intently turning the pages of his book about the pioneers of skateboarding culture. When he's not hanging out with me and Grace, Luis is skateboarding every chance he gets. Ms. Tremt really does have a knack for putting the right books into our hands.

We're deep into our reading when a loud *thud* startles us. I must be daydreaming, because I look up and for a moment I can swear I see star Brooklyn Dodgers baseball player Jackie Robinson in his 1951 Dodgers uniform smiling at me and tossing a baseball in the corner of the library. I must be overtired, though. It's only Ms. Tremt dropping a box of books—another box of books!—onto our table. But this box isn't like the other boxes in the room. Those boxes are just ordinary cardboard ones. *This* box is as interesting as one of Ms. Tremt's scarves, but a whole lot heavier. It's golden, maybe brass? Definitely not cardboard. And there are strange things carved all over it—not exactly pictures, more like writing (if the letters of the alphabet looked like scribbles, that is). Also the latch of the box is held closed by a set of gears that will turn when you crank a tiny handle.

"Luis. Grace. Matthew." Ms. Tremt says, looking each one of us in the eyes. "I need some assistance after school today. Can you spare some time for me?"

"Sorry, Ms. Tremt, I have a big play-off game later," I apologize. "I can come tomorrow."

"Oh, Matthew, I know all about your game," Ms. Tremt says. "You'll still be able to make it. It's one little box to unpack. How long could it take?"

"We'll be here," Grace replies for the three of us with a smile.

I can feel Luis kicking the both of us under the table. Grace kicks back even harder, and gives Luis the Look.

"Okay. We'll be here, Ms. Tremt," Luis says obediently. "You can count on us."

"I knew you'd make time for me." Ms. Tremt smiles. "Thank you."

"Oh, and please," Ms. Tremt adds, "try not to peek in the box before then."

Oh no! Ms. Tremt is obviously not aware of what she has just done to Luis "Curiosity-may-kill-cats-but-it-will-never-get-me" Ramirez. I look over and see Ms. Tremt's eyes set on Luis the way I set my eyes on a catcher's mitt. Hmmm. Maybe Ms. Tremt is aware of what Luis will surely do next.

Just then we hear an ear-piercing scream coming from the back of the library. Two Vikings—yes, you heard me right, Vikings, in full Viking gear, helmets with horns and shields and swords—suddenly charge through the library screaming and yelling and throwing books at each other.

"Aaaargh! You stole my furs and tusks!" one bellows.

"Aaaargh, you stole my seal fat!" the second screams back. "For that you must die!" All the kids in the library gasp and start yelling too. I look at Ms. Tremt, who's suddenly a bit pale. She says, "Nothing to be afraid of, children—it's just part of a play I'm directing after school." She walks over to the two men, looks them straight in the eyes, and says calmly, "Gentlemen! This way, please," and amazingly, they both clam up and quietly follow her out of the library. Before she leaves, she turns to the three of us again, and says, "Remember, try not to peek in that box."

I look at Luis and Grace. Grace seems to take the Viking actors in stride, but Luis thinks it's the funniest thing he's seen in quite a while.

"Yaaah! Give me your seal fat, Matt!" he yells. "And if you don't have any, then hand over that chicken parm sandwich your mom made you for lunch!" He laughs at his own joke, then turns his attention back to the box Ms. Tremt left with us.

I see the sparkle in Luis's eyes and know that box is going to be open in five seconds flat.

CHAPTER	TITLE
2	Page-Turner

The library suddenly seems even more hushed than usual. So quiet that the sound of Luis's fingers tapping the box is practically thunderous.

"Don't even think about it, dude," I whisper to Luis.

"Think about what?" Luis says, the corners of his mouth turning up into a grin. He knows that I know exactly what he's thinking.

I spy Luis's fingers creeping up toward the tiny handle as he looks around the room to see what Ms. Tremt is doing.

"Stop!" I whisper-hiss. "She said not to open the box."

"Actually, she said, '*Try* not to peek,'" Luis says snarkily. "I tried. I failed. Now I will peek."

Just then, I feel a kick under the table and see that Grace is giving *me* the Look. Me!

"Um, Grace, I think your kick was meant for someone else," I whisper.

"She did say 'try,'" Grace whispers back. "Just 'try.' She didn't forbid us from looking."

I guess Grace is Luis's new partner on Team Curiosity. Who am I to stop them, anyway?

Luis takes a glance around the library to make certain Ms. Tremt is nowhere in sight, and then quickly ducks under the table with the box. He nimbly turns the tiny handle. The gears spin, and after a few turns, and the latch clicks.

"Let me open it!" Grace says as she ducks under the table too, knocking a stack of books with her elbow. I quickly scoop them up before they hit the floor.

"Or . . . maybe you should do it, Luis," Grace whispers.

"Good thinking," Luis says.

I can't help it, the curiosity seems to be contagious, so I duck down to get a look too. Luis opens the cover of the box and pulls out the first book he can grab. .

The book is dusty, thick, and heavy—heavier than the baseball almanacs Grandpa Joe likes to drag out on rainy days. The cover feels like the soft leather of my baseball glove, but it has a shimmer that isn't quite gold, isn't quite silver . . . it's some other substance that I can't actually pinpoint. The letters of the title are raised on the cover in dark black ink, the black of a moonless midnight sky.

"*The Book of Memories,*" Grace reads aloud. "Interesting. I wonder whose memories they are?"

"Let's find out," Luis says as he carefully holds the front cover in one hand and uses the other to open it to a parchment page gilded with gold leaf. Grace softly reads the words on the first page like prayer.

> "*TO SIGN OUT THIS*
> *BOOK REQUIRES SPECIAL*
> *PERMISSION.*

PLEASE SEE LIBRARIAN
VALERIE TREMT."

Luis peeks his head up from under the table. Ms. Tremt is back behind her desk, and the Vikings are nowhere in sight. "I see Librarian Valerie Tremt," Luis jokes. "Does that give me permission?"

"No, it does not," Grace replies sternly. "But look, this is odd."

Like I just said, the book is thick, and it obviously has a whole bunch of gilded pages between its covers, but when Grace tries to flip past the first page, it doesn't budge. Not even a smidge. Then Luis tries. And I try. Nothing.

"Enough with the book already, okay?" I plead with my friends. "It looks really old, and it's probably valuable. I don't want to get in trouble."

"Agreed," Grace replies. "Who knows what it is. Maybe it's something really private—like Ms. Tremt's diary that got mixed in with these books by mistake! We'll just have to ask her about it later, when we come back to help."

"All right." I sigh. "But don't ask *too* much

about it. Today's a big day for me. Baseball game, star pitcher, remember?"

The rest of the day is filled with typical middle school stuff. Here's my Wednesday schedule. If you're interested, you can fill in the unexciting dots from there. (Or skip over it, if you want. I wish I could, but I've gotta run to math class.)

Wednesday

8:00–8:50   Library/Ms. Tremt

8:55–9:45   Math/Mr. Bodon

9:50–10:40   English/Mr. Wiley

10:45–11:35 Science Lab/Mrs. Kokotas

11:40–12:30 LUNCH

12:35–1:25   History/Ms. Castine

1:30–2:20   Study Island

When the final bell rings, I rush to the boys' locker room and quickly change into my baseball uniform. I'm no Boy Scout, but I do know to always be prepared, especially for a big game. And if I know Grace and Luis, this is going to take a lot longer than the fifteen minutes it should take to unpack a box of books. The game starts at 3:30. It's 2:30 now, and I'd like to leave by 3:00 at the very latest.

Ms. Tremt is waiting at the library doors. I'm a little confused. I can't possibly be the first one to arrive. Luis and Grace didn't even have to get changed.

"A quick word, Matthew," Ms. Tremt says as if she is about to tell me a secret.

"Yes, Ms. Tremt?" I reply.

"I know you're concerned you'll be late for your game, and worried that this is going to take longer than you expected," she continues. "You have nothing to worry about. I am a most excellent manager of time."

"That's good to know," I say. "Can we get started, though?"

"Of course." Ms. Tremt laughs. "Your friends

are already here and waiting for you."

I can tell right away that something is up when Ms. Tremt and I walk through the door. Grace walks over, her head down and her hands behind her back. A guilty stance if I ever saw one. I knew being a member of Team Curiosity would get to her.

"Ms. Tremt," Grace says as she brings her hands forward and holds out *The Book of Memories*. "I think you gave us this book by accident. Well . . . not exactly 'gave,' but, um . . ."

I know Grace is trying to tell Ms. Tremt about the book, but her stumbling makes me uncomfortable. She's going to make us all look guilty. Luckily, Ms. Tremt doesn't seem concerned at all.

"Nothing in library time is an accident, dear," she reassures Grace. "Are you interested in the book? I knew you would be."

Grace's uncomfortable grimace instantly turns into a wide grin.

"Soooo interested," she gushes. "It's the most beautiful book I've ever seen. I just wish there were some actual pages to read."

Ms. Tremt laughs, and it sounds strangely like wind chimes echoing off the bookshelves.

"There *are* actual pages, Grace," she replies. "You'll get to them—in due time."

Grace moves forward to hand the book to Ms. Tremt, but trips over my cleat and *The Book of Memories* flips from her hands, flies through the air, and plops onto Ms. Tremt's desk. *Thud!*

"Sorry, Ms. Tremt!" Grace says.

"It's high time the dust was knocked off that book." Ms. Tremt laughs. "You did me a favor."

"And what about you, Matt?" Ms. Tremt asks as she turns to me. "Are you interested in my book?"

"Well, honestly, I probably would be, but you know, big game and all," I say, still trying to get out of there as quickly as possible.

"Ms. Tremt!" Luis shouts from behind me, nearly blowing out my eardrums. "ME! ME! ME! I'm interested!"

I turn and see that he is waving his hand furiously up and down like a little kid in class who knows the answer to one plus one, and doesn't realize that almost everyone else in the class knows it too. I roll my eyes at him.

Ms. Tremt pats him on the back and chuckles. "*That* is not a surprise, Luis. But I'll tell you what—there are some mysteries you three need to unlock first."

"Like how I'm going to get to my game on time," I huff.

"On time, on shmime," Ms. Tremt replies. "If you solve these mysteries, you'll have all the time in the world in your hands."

"Okay, great. What are the clues?" I say, ready to wrap this up.

"One of the clues is right in front of you," Ms. Tremt says. "Me!"

"You definitely are a mystery, Ms. Tremt," Luis says, grinning. "But can we get another clue? Pretty please?"

"Of course," Ms. Tremt answers. "Everything about me, Valerie Tremt, is a clue."

Ms. Tremt carefully picks up *The Book of Memories* from the desk and opens a drawer. She gently places the book in the drawer and closes it. I watch as she uses an unusually shaped, old-fashioned key to lock the drawer. The top of the key looks like a stopwatch. Then she turns away from us and begins shelving some of the stacks of books.

Luis, Grace, and I head back to our table.

"What was that all about?" I whisper to my friends.

Grace stares at Ms. Tremt as if she's a biologist studying a newly discovered species. "She said, 'Everything about me, Valerie Tremt, is a clue.'"

"Yes, she did," I say. "So what do we know about her?"

Luis shrugs. "She's smart. She likes books. Her clothes are kind of interesting."

"That's an understatement," I say with a laugh.

"She must love old things," Grace adds. "I noticed she uses a really old fountain pen—the kind you have to fill up with ink."

"And that old-fashioned key," I remind her. "But a lot of people like antiques. That can't be the clue. Why did she say, 'Everything about me, Valerie Tremt, is a clue'? She could have just said, 'Everything about me is a clue.'"

"Good point," Grace says. "That might be a clue."

23

Have I mentioned how much I hate mysteries? 'Cause I do. Just give me the fastball, straight and over the plate. I might swing and miss, but at least I know where you're coming from. I have no idea where in the world Ms. Tremt is coming from. But I guess we're going to have to find that out, because I know Grace and Luis aren't giving up on this puzzle any time soon.

Suddenly I hear giggling. I look up and everyone in the library is nudging one another and pointing. What are they looking at? I turn around and see a guy who looks exactly like Albert Einstein holding a book and frowning. He walks over to Jeffrey Tyler, who's in my science class. The guy in the Albert Einstein costume tosses the book he's holding down on the table in front of Jeffrey.

"Unauthorized nonsense!" he yells. He opens the book and points to a specific page. "I never said any of this when I was developing my theories of relativity. Jeffrey, please make sure you do not use this book as a source when you write your report. I will not be misquoted. Is that clear?"

Jeffrey looks up, both shocked and fearful,

and gives a little nod. Then Einstein guy almost immediately cheers up. He smiles at Jeffrey and says, "And by the way, don't worry about being shy. I didn't speak until I was four years old! And look how I turned out!"

At this point Ms. Tremt rushes over. She grabs the guy by the sleeve and says, "Come with me, Albert." She turns to the students in the library and says, "Another actor, children! Nothing for you to concern yourselves with! Carry on!"

Meanwhile, Jeffrey turns to me in a daze and says, "I'm writing a book report about Einstein. He's my idol. That guy looked exactly like him, didn't he? But how did he know I was writing a report about Einstein? And how did he know I was shy?"

Grace, Luis, and I all stare at one another. What in the world is going on with Ms. Tremt and the library at Sands Middle School?

CHAPTER	TITLE
3	The First Step

Okay, I don't have time to worry about Albert Einstein or people dressed up like him running through the library. It's already 3:05 and my game starts at 3:30. I remind Grace and Luis how important "soon" is right now. *I have to leave soon, guys. My game is starting soon. Hey, can the mystery wait until later? Because I need to leave soon.*

Okay, maybe I remind them more than a few times. Unfortunately, Grace and Luis just don't seem to have the same sense of urgency that I do.

And Ms. Tremt, well, she's on a totally different schedule, that's for sure.

"In case you missed the lesson," I say, trying to be funny, but really feeling anxious and dead serious. "*Soon*. The definition is 'a time that is not long from now.' Or not long from fifteen minutes ago, which is when I told you that I needed to leave SOON. Seriously, the mystery can wait!"

"Relax," Grace says. "The answer to the mystery is right here, Matt, I know it is. We just need to find it. Then you can go."

Grace sounds just like my coaches. *Relax. No pressure, Matt. Take a deep breath.* Which is easy to say when you're not standing on the mound, facing a twelve-year-old hulking over home plate who's already over six feet tall and has more facial hair than Grandpa Joe. Easy for Grace to say, when she doesn't have to be on that mound *soon*.

I sigh heavily and stare at Ms. Tremt at her desk. For some reason my eyes are drawn to her nameplate. Valerie Tremt. Valerie Tremt. I stare at it for so long the letters almost seem to dance in front of my eyes. I turn to Grace and see she's staring at it too. I'm pretty sure we're thinking the same thing. *Everything about me, Valerie Tremt, is a clue. . . .*

"Hey, check it out," Luis's voice interrupts our thoughts. "Do you see what Ms. Tremt is doing?"

Fountain pen in hand, Ms. Tremt is furiously jotting down letters on a piece of scrap paper. On her desk is a book titled *Jumbo Jumble*. All of a sudden her fountain pen begins to emit a glowing green light. As we walk toward the desk, it starts to blink and flash.

"Cool light-up pen, Ms. Tremt," I say.

Ms. Tremt smiles. "The flashing is actually a sign that you are close to what you need to know. Time is on your side. Make the most of it."

The flashing what . . . ? But I don't really have time to ponder what Ms. Tremt could possibly mean because three seconds after she stops talking, Grace gasps and grabs my arm. She takes hold of Luis's arm with her other hand and nearly carries us back to the table. Of course, in Grace's gentle but clumsy hands, we are like a three-friend wrecking machine. Our entwined arms hit one stack of books— *BLAM!* There goes another—*BOOM!* One more for good luck—*CRASH!*

"Don't worry," Ms. Tremt calls to us. "I can stack those later. Carry on."

I have no idea what lightbulb moment Grace has just had, but her brain is clearly on overdrive and she can't wait to tell us her thoughts.

"It's an anagram!" she whispers.

"A what-a-gram?" I say.

"Her name!" Grace says. "It's an anagram. A word jumble!"

Grace pulls out a pen and paper from her knapsack and starts to fill the page with letters.

I take a peek at the paper. In the middle, written in large block letters, is the name VALERIE TREMT. Scribbled all around it are different letter combinations.

REAL METER VIT

ATELTEM RIVER

RELATIVE TERM

TIME TRAVELER

Grace taps her pen excitedly on the last one. She underlines it. Then she circles it. Then she starts drawing little stars all around the circle.

Luis leans in and takes a look. A huge grin breaks out on his face. "Are you kidding me?" he says. "No way! But . . . maybe! That might explain some of the weird stuff that's been going on in here today."

I have no idea what they are talking about.

"I'm sorry, am I missing something?" I ask. "Because, as you know, I have a big game starting very soo—"

"Matt!" Grace huffs. "Get your mind off the mound already! Valerie Tremt is an anagram for 'time traveler'!"

I take Grace's pen from her hand and start to cross off the letters in "Valerie Tremt" as I spell out "time traveler" in my head. She's right!

Ms. Tremt is standing right behind me before I've even crossed out the last *T*.

"It's about time you figured it out!" She laughs. "Yes, I am a time traveler. Now follow me. There's something I want to show you."

Ms. Tremt leads us to a door hidden in the

wall at the back corner of the library. She opens the door with the same old-fashioned key she used to lock her desk drawer. All four of us walk into an empty classroom.

"I never knew this room existed," Grace says. "What are we doing here?"

"Getting ready to have the time of your lives," Ms. Tremt replies.

Grace's eyes widen and she smiles like it's Christmas morning.

I look at Luis and we roll our eyes at each other. Clearly, Grace has bought into the time-traveler thing completely. I think the whole anagram puzzle is kind of cool, but come on. Ms. Tremt, a time traveler? Luis and I live in the real world. Grace and our librarian seem to have spent a little too much time with fiction. Science fiction, in particular.

"Dr. Who, nice to meet you," Luis jokes.

"No, wait, Ms. Tremt is more like Meg Murry," I say. "From *A Wrinkle in Time*."

"Dude, think about the possibilities," Luis says. "First we could go back in time and save President Lincoln!"

"And then President Kennedy!" I add.

"Then we'll win a few lottery jackpots!" Luis suggests.

"Sweet!" I reply.

"Enough, boys," Ms. Tremt says sternly. "I know you think you're joking about fantastical impossibilities . . . and you are. You can't do *any* of those things when you travel through time."

And then Ms. Tremt proceeds to tell us a bunch of rules about time travel as if they're actually true.

"You can't change major events in history," she continues. "And time will not allow you to act for purely selfish reasons. You can't go back and pick the right lottery numbers, or bet on the winning World Series team."

"Why not?" Grace asks seriously.

"Time portals are powered by positive energy," Ms. Tremt adds. "And time is an elastic dimension. Therefore, not all minutes are created equally. In time, positive energy is stronger than negative energy."

"I'm not sure I understand what you're talking about," I admit.

"Me either," Luis pipes up. "This is some serious mind-blowing, time-bending stuff you're talking about here!"

"It simply means that time travel is just another potential reality, but one that must align with all past and all future events, positively," Ms. Tremt explains. "You may choose to surf the ridges of time, Matt. And if you do, then what you *can* do is make a change—one single, small change for the good—in your family's personal history. You can create a positive effect for your inner family circle, but that effect cannot impact the persistence of time."

Luis looks around the classroom skeptically.

"So where's the Tardis? The Tesseract?" he asks. "You know, the time-traveling device?"

Ms. Tremt holds up *The Book of Memories*. "Ta-daaa! Here you go, Luis."

Now I know Ms. Tremt is acting.

"You really had me for a minute there," I tell her. "You made it all sound so real."

"That's because it is," Ms. Tremt says. "I would never, ever joke about time."

"So where's your handy-dandy zapper?" Luis

asks. "You know, the one you use to shrink us so we can jump into the book?"

"I don't have one, Luis." Ms. Tremt laughs. "That's not the way it works. Time is literally in your hands when you hold this book."

Grace, who has been mentally taking notes the whole time, snuggles up to Ms. Tremt's side as the librarian opens the book to the title page. There's a little card where you write your name and date to sign the book out, like the ones in the old books before our school library started using barcodes and scanners. Now everything is computerized. I wonder why we didn't notice that when we first opened the book.

Ms. Tremt pulls her trusty fountain pen from her pocket and signs her name on the card.

Magically, the book begins to sparkle with the same green glow as Ms. Tremt's fountain pen. The glow swirls around the page until it stops, forming a sentence. Grace, Luis, and I read it aloud.

"'Where would you like to go today?'"

No way! I did not just see that! I blink a few times, then I rub my eyes, but the green glowing words are still there.

"So, where *would* you like to go today?" Ms. Tremt says. "For demonstration purposes only, of course."

I guess Luis is starting to take this seriously as well, because he's the first to speak.

"Matt, what were our favorite things in preschool?" he asks. "I'll give you a hint. My favorite was a Triceratops. Yours was a T. rex."

"Dinosaurs?" I say, remembering the hours we spent in preschool playing with toy dinosaur figurines.

"Exactly!" Luis cheers. "I've always wanted to see one up close. . . . Haven't you?"

"Well, I'm not sure how up close I'd want to get to a T. rex," I admit. "But yeah, it would be cool."

"An excellent—yet dangerous—choice," Ms. Tremt notes. "It's high time we got prehistoric. We shall travel back sixty-five million years."

Huh? I'm not ready to agree to anything here. I mean, sure, I am a little curious, but what if this isn't all just an act. What if science fiction isn't fiction at all?

"The Mesozoic Era," Ms. Tremt says as she

writes it in the book with her fountain pen. "Same geographical coordinates as present." She smiles at us. "This is one library book you're allowed to write in," she says.

Nothing happens. Honestly, it's a relief.

"Well, it's been fun, Ms. Tremt, but I don't have time for magic tricks right now," I say as I try to make a quick exit from the room. But before I can get to the door, Ms. Trempt closes *The Book of Memories* and places it against the wall.

"Don't move, Matt," she warns.

The book begins to shake.

And stretch.

And grow.

Higher and higher, wider and wider, until it fills the entire wall like a giant mural.

"Now you may open the book," Ms. Tremt declares.

So we do. Come on, you know you would be curious too!

Remember the last time, when we tried to open the book, but we couldn't? Well, now imagine that when we open the book, instead of a title page we see a full-color 3-D image of a prehistoric landscape that is filling the wall of a classroom you never even knew existed in your school. And that in the middle of that landscape is one of those tiny toy dinosaurs you used to play with (or still do). Except that it isn't tiny at all, and it isn't a toy, either. It's a life-size, totally real Tyrannosaurus rex.

Still, I'm not quite ready to become a true believer yet. I mean, classroom technology can be pretty amazing these days. Maybe it's just some new brand of Smart Board that Ms. Tremt is testing. That has to be it.

Except it isn't.

"As I said, this is just for demonstration purposes," Ms. Tremt informs us. "So you're not actually going to *go* to the Mesozoic Era. But observe."

The next moment is the one in which I become a true believer. Right before my eyes, when Ms. Tremt walks over to the wall and touches the scene, her hand disappears into the wall and appears inside the image!

The T. rex notices her hand and starts to charge toward it.

"Ms. Tremt!" Luis, Grace, and I scream simultaneously.

"If I wanted to, I could go into this time period, via this image," she explains, her hand now back in the classroom.

Grace leans forward, trying to get a closer look. But Grace being Grace, she loses her balance and nearly knocks Ms. Tremt completely into the photo. She was just about to crash into the T. rex, but Luis and I grab her and pull her back just in time. We all watch as the dinosaur looks around in confusion and then trudges off.

"Sorry, Ms. Tremt," Grace says timidly.

"No worries, Grace," Ms. Tremt says. "That wasn't my first time getting a little too close to a dinosaur, but it's never fun. Thank you, boys."

It's hard for me to wrap my brain around what I just witnessed. But then I see Luis get a funny look on his face.

"Waaaaaait a minute, Ms. Tremt," he says. "Those guys you said were actors before? The Vikings, Albert Einstein . . ."

"Those weren't actors, Luis," Ms. Tremt tells him. "Because of the power of *The Book of*

Memories, sometimes things can get a little wacky in this library. For example, when a student is concentrating especially hard, their thoughts have been known to break the time-space continuum, and people from the past randomly appear. Fortunately, so far I've been able to catch them and bring them back where they belong before they cause too much trouble."

"Hold on, hold on, HOLD ON!" I shout. "You mean that was the *real* Jackie Robinson I saw this morning? He was *here*? In *my* school? And I didn't talk to him? Bring him back, *bring him back*!"

Ms. Tremt laughs. "Not today, Matthew. Another time, perhaps."

A memory from a few months ago flashes through my mind. I was helping Grace with her report on Martin Luther King Jr. We didn't think much of it at the time, but I'm now remembering a man who looked exactly like Dr. King talking to Ms. Tremt. The suit he was wearing even matched the one on the cover of Grace's book. But just like Einstein and the Vikings, Ms. Tremt immediately escorted him out of the library. I shake my head. This is all too much to believe. Too much!

"Now, mind you, I could stay in the Mesozoic Era for precisely three hours," she adds. "After which, I would just need to sign the book back to the present time. Then I would be delivered here, to this library, safe and sound. No time will have passed in the present. I will return to the exact moment and place I left. It's the ultimate time-share."

"Why?" Luis asks.

"Because it's a time-travel device," Ms. Tremt says patiently.

"But why?" Luis persists.

"*Why?*" Ms. Tremt echoes, sounding a little more impatient than usual. "Luis, you do realize I just showed you a book that is a portal to the past. It breaks the time-space continuum. This could be Nobel Prize–winning, *New York Times* front-page news. If I explain all the details to you until you understand, Matt will never get to his game. So let's just agree that it *does* work. Why is the sky blue, Luis?"

"Because the light refracts—" Grace begins.

"Thank you, Grace." Ms. Tremt smiles. "I'm sure your answer is scientifically accurate and would enlighten Luis greatly. But my question was meant to be rhetorical."

"Oops, my bad." Grace giggles.

Ms. Tremt continues, "I chose you three for a reason. On the outside you may seem wildly different, but you have stayed friends because of your similarities. You are all smart. Funny. Kind. You care about the world around you. And, in a way you can't fully understand yet, you are all ahead of your time. That's why I am offering each of you this chance to change one small thing. This particular adventure is for Matt. But Grace and Luis, don't worry. I assure you, you both will also get your opportunity in due time."

"One small thing . . . ," Grace repeats.

"One small thing that would make everything different," Luis says thoughtfully.

I still can't believe this is actually happening, but I'm as sure of what I want to say next as I am when throwing my cutter to a batter with two strikes against him.

"I know exactly where and when I want to go,

41

Ms. Tremt," I say. "Bay Ridge, Brooklyn, New York. July 4, 1951."

Grace and Luis look at each other and grin. They totally know why I chose that particular day.

Ms. Tremt smiles and seems curious, but I have a hard time believing she didn't know where I would want to go all along. Just a funny feeling I have.

"Why July 4, 1951, Matt?" she asks anyway. "What would going back to that long-ago Fourth of July change for you?"

"Grandpa Joe is finally going to become a Major League ballplayer," I say.

Words have never sounded better leaving my mouth.

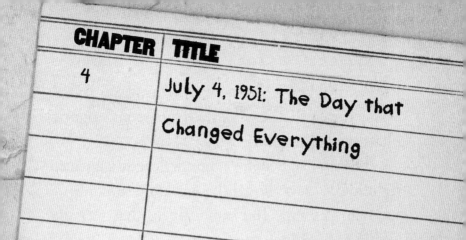

I could recite the story of the pool party on July 4, 1951, in my sleep. So can Grace and Luis, it seems. They jump in and start to tell Ms. Tremt all the details. I keep my mouth shut and just give Ms. Tremt a knowing smile. *Sure you don't know the story, Ms. Tremt. Sure you don't.*

"Matt's grandpa was a great baseball player," Luis says. "Still is. Well, definitely a better one than I am."

"He's smart, too!" Grace adds. "He got a scholarship to an expensive prep school in Bay

Ridge, Brooklyn. And he was a star player there. So good that the New York Giants scout stopped by to check him out."

"He was signed to a minor league contract right away, even though he was only seventeen," Luis chimes in. "The same spring that teenage Willie Mays joined the Giants!"

"Grandpa Joe was sure to get called up to the majors in September 1951," Grace goes on. "He had the hottest bat on the Blue Angels high school team. Not only that, he was an amazing pitcher. Everyone knew he was going to make it to the show."

Oh man! You know Gracie's been hanging out at my house too long when she starts calling the major leagues "the show"! She sounds just like Grandpa Joe. Grace continues the story.

"So on July Fourth, Matt's grandpa is on top of the world. And, you know, one of the perks of going to a prep school is that you get to make friends who live a little better than you might. Like Grandpa Joe's best friend, Alex. Alex had a pool in his backyard, which was practically unheard of at the time. Of course, it helped that the backyard was in one of the richest sections of Brooklyn."

I jump in to finish the tale. I want to move forward—or actually backward—already.

"He started the day on top of the world, but it all came crashing down at the party," I say sadly.

"You don't have to go on," Ms. Tremt interrupts. "I can figure out the rest myself. Grandpa Joe didn't make it to the show."

"No, he didn't," I finish, trying to not sound as sad as the story always made me. "He hurt his ankle at the party. . . . It was worse than he thought. His contract with the Giants was canceled."

"One small thing," I say, remembering Ms. Tremt's words. "If I can prevent Grandpa's accident from happening, he'd become a Major League Baseball player. It's a small thing. My whole life I've heard him say if he could just take back those five minutes, his whole life would be different. I'd love to give him that chance to fulfill his dream."

When I look down, I see Ms. Tremt's fountain pen is glowing again.

"Matt, your time-travel request has been approved," she tells me. "When my pen glows, it means your intentions are good, and you will be able to travel to whatever time period you would like to go to. So when would you like to leave?"

"Um, right now?" I say. "July 4, 1951! Give me that pen, I'm ready to sign this book out!"

"Slow down, Matt." Ms. Tremt laughs. "As a French philosopher once said, 'Those who make the worst use of their time are the first to complain of its brevity.' Remember, *The Book of Memories* only grants you three hours in the past, and three hours is not long at all. You'll have a much better chance at success if you think your journey through before you depart."

"Yeah, Matt," Luis adds. "Think about it. Are we just going to show up at the party and say, 'Hey, Joe, we're from the future. Be careful today, or you're gonna ruin your life'?"

"What's wrong with that?" I ask. "It might work!" Grace gives me the Look again.

"We really do need a game plan, Matt," she says. "You should know that better than anyone."

"Take tonight to think it over," Ms. Tremt

advises. "I'll start the necessary preparations for your journey tomorrow."

Then Ms. Tremt looks at her watch. "Soon has finally arrived, Matt. You'd better hurry. Your baseball game is about to start shortly."

I looked at Ms. Tremt and sighed. "Start? My game must be half over by now. We've been here for . . ." I look at my phone but can't believe my eyes. "Ten minutes?! But, Ms. Tremt, it feels like we've been here for hours!"

"May I remind you, Matt, I am an excellent manager of time," our librarian replies with a smile.

My game goes super well. We win 4–3, thanks in part to my pitching three scoreless innings and hitting a double that brought in the winning run. Of course Grace and Luis come to watch and cheer me on, and then they invite themselves over for dinner. I know Grandpa Joe won't mind, since it's usually the four of us—my grandpa, my grandma, me, and my mom—and he likes having a crowd around to listen to his stories.

He likes it even more because dinner for four

is often dinner for three—Mom's almost always stuck at work late and usually can't join us for dinner. And Grandma cooks for an army, every meal. She jokes and says it's an Italian thing. I think it's a grandma thing.

I don't want to be super obvious, but I can't help pummeling Grandpa with questions as soon as we sit down to eat. Ms. Tremt is right—I need to know as much as I can about the day of the accident.

"Grandpa, tell me again about the Fourth of July when you hurt your leg," I say as I scoop a swirl of spaghetti into my mouth.

"Why do you want to hear that story again?" Grandpa Joe asks, surprised.

"I asked him about it today," Grace pipes up.

I'm grateful. I know Grace has also heard the story too many times, but Grandpa doesn't know that. He just thinks Grace is curious.

Grandpa Joe puts down his fork and sighs. It's like a lifetime of disappointment floats on that exhalation.

"I felt like the sky was the limit," Grandpa Joe begins. "All I ever wanted to do was play

48

baseball. I loved everything about the game—the smell of fresh-cut grass in the outfield, the feel of the weight of a hickory bat, the sound of the thud the ball made when it landed in leather. I still love it."

"Anyway," my grandfather continues. "It was supposed to be a great day. The Giants scout said I was sure to get a call up soon. And my best friend, Alex, was throwing the biggest party of the summer. Patty Caravale—that's your great aunt Patty, Matt—was at the party, and she looked so pretty. I had a crush on her for the longest time. When her favorite song came on the radio, I knew it was time to make a move."

"What song was it?" Luis asks.

Grandpa Joe grins. "'Ballerina.' I used to love the way Nat King Cole sang that!"

My grandma hums the melody as she puts a plate of meatballs and sausage on the table in front of Grandpa Joe.

"Patty was studying ballet," she says. "Remember, Joe, there's a line in the song 'Twirl, ballerina, twirl . . .'"

Grandpa Joe finishes her sentence, "Yes, and I was twirling Matt's great aunt Patty a little too close to the pool steps. Neither one of us was paying attention and . . . well, it wasn't a pretty picture. My ankle was never the same after that fall. It was okay for most things, but baseball was out of the question."

"Wait, I'm confused. Who is Matt's great aunt Patty?" Grace asks.

"My older sister, Patty Caravale," Grandma Jeanie explains.

"And I'll owe her forever," Grandpa Joe adds. "I wouldn't have met the love of my life if it wasn't for her. When Patty came to visit me after I hurt my ankle, she brought her baby sister along. Now Patty may have been pretty, but with Jeanie here, well, it was love at first sight. The minute I saw her, I knew she was the girl I was going to marry. So even though it ended my baseball career, something wonderful came out of that July Fourth."

"Aw, Joe." Grandma Jeanie sighs as she pats his hand. "Sometimes I still wish we had met under different circumstances. Like cheering for you playing for the Giants."

"Who are you kidding?" Grandpa laughs. "You, me, and everyone else we knew were Brooklyn Dodgers fans. It would have been a crime to cheer for the Giants!"

"Well, I'd have been cheering on the inside if you were on the team," Grandma admits.

"Did Patty ever become a ballerina?" Grace asks.

"Not professionally," Grandma Jeanie says. "She got married, moved to California, and had three kids. But she did open a dance school out there."

"And where was Uncle Alex when you fell?" I ask.

"Who knows?" Grandpa Joe answers. "Do you know how many people were at that party? It was a madhouse!"

"Wait," Luis says, shooting me a look. "So there were people at the party Alex didn't even know?"

"Sure," Grandpa Joe replies. "It was a different time. We didn't have texts or tweets or fancy phones, but believe me, back then, when there was a good party going on, word spread faster than a viral video."

Luis, Grace, and I look at one another knowingly. Now we don't have to worry about getting invited to the party. We can walk right in!

I help Grandma clean up and load the dishwasher, and then I say good-bye to my friends. I know I should probably get some sleep, but my mind just refuses to shut down. I sit down at my computer and search the Internet for a map of Brooklyn, print it out to give to Ms. Tremt, and mark key landmarks. I put a star on the most important one—Uncle Alex's house—8107 Bay Vista Drive.

Time starts to play tricks on me. The night races by as I think about my plans. *What will I say when I first see my grandfather in 1951? What should I wear? I'd better ask Ms. Tremt. Are there any other "time-traveling rules" we should know about?* Just when I'm finally about to doze off, it's time to head to school. But then the seconds of the school day are never-ending! It seems like decades between the first and final bells of the day.

The instant the final bell rings, Luis, Grace, and I rush to the library. Ms. Tremt is waiting with a huge crate.

"First things first," she says. "You all have to look the part. You need to blend in."

Ms. Tremt pulls out a box labeled GRACE from the crate.

"For me?" Grace coos as she opens her box. Then her face falls.

"What is it?" I ask. "What?"

Grace pulls out a long, swirly skirt complete with a big pink embroidered poodle. Luis and I both crack up. "No way." Grace says, stuffing the skirt back in the box. "No."

"Come on!" Ms. Tremt says. "You'll look adorable in it!"

"No," Grace says definitively. "N-O."

"Oh well, I tried." Ms. Tremt sighs, tossing one of her furry scarves over her shoulder. "Fortunately, I was prepared for some pushback."

There's a second box labeled GRACE. Inside is a simple black skirt, a plain white shirt, black-and-white shoes, and short white socks.

"Okay, now this I can work with," Grace says, relieved.

"The black-and-white shoes are called 'saddle shoes,'" Ms. Tremt explains. "And they were the height of teenage fashion in the fifties. And the short socks were called 'bobby socks.' You might have heard the expression 'bobby soxers'—it is what people called girls who wore saddle shoes and bobby socks and swooned over their favorite singers, like Frank Sinatra or Elvis Presley."

"Will we meet any Elvis fans in 1951?" Luis asks excitedly. "My grandma loved Elvis!"

"No," Ms. Tremt tells us. "Elvis was unheard of in 1951. He didn't become popular until 1956. And now, Matt, Luis, here are some clothes for both of you."

Now it's time for *our* fashion trip through time. We open our boxes and high-five. Jeans and T-shirts, not bad at all. The main difference is that the jeans have cuffs. The shoes are another story—they look like fancy leather dress shoes. But as long as no one is taking pictures and bringing them back to the present day, I can live with them.

"I have to wear a whole new outfit and all you two need to do is wear leather shoes and cuff your jeans," Grace complains. "Not fair!"

Then Grace looks at Luis's long shaggy hair and smiles.

"He's probably going to have to cut his hair, though. Right, Ms. Tremt?"

"Not a chance. I'm not cutting it," Luis says.

Ms. Tremt hands him a jar of styling gel.

"Just slick it back," she advises. "You'll be fine for a three-hour trip."

Luis and I head to the boys' bathroom to change. Grace, obviously, goes to the girls' bathroom.

When we meet outside in the hall, two kids passing by look at us as if we've each sprouted another head.

"School project," Luis mumbles to them, embarrassed.

Ms. Tremt thinks we look perfect, though.

"Just a couple of things to review," she says. "First, some basic rules."

Grace whips out her pen and pad and takes notes.

"Be sure to limit your interactions with people from the past," Ms. Tremt says. "Always keep in mind that any little thing you say has the potential to change the future drastically."

Wow, I totally did not think of that. I grab

Grace's pen and draw a big star next to that note.

"Also, do not reference anything that was invented or created after 1951—*under any circumstances!*" Ms. Tremt warns.

She hands us each a wristwatch, the old-school kind with a wind-up side dial, and then holds out the crate. It's time to empty our pockets of all electronic devices. Bye-bye, smartphone! See you on the flip side.

"I always make sure my time travelers have a watch that is appropriate for their time period," Ms. Tremt explains.

"Now, hand over any money you three are carrying," Ms. Tremt demands.

"My money?" Luis says, baffled. "Didn't they have cash back in 1951, Ms. Tremt?"

"They did, Luis, but how are you going to explain . . ." She grabs a dollar bill that Luis has taken from his pocket and holds it up to the light. "A dollar bill issued in 2016?"

Ms. Tremt is time-travel smart, that's for sure. Another thing I would never have thought of on my own. Ms. Tremt puts all our cash in the crate, then hands us each a stack of bills.

"What the what?" Luis protests. "I gave you thirty dollars, and you're giving me five dollars back in exchange? Did you forget to read math books? That was my birthday money, Ms. Tremt!"

"Luis, I do appreciate your insatiable curiosity, but sometimes you are just going to have to trust me," she tells him. "In 1951, minimum wage was seventy-five cents an hour. You simply cannot be seen walking around with the equivalent of an adult's weekly salary as pocket money. Naturally you'll get all your cash back upon your return to the present."

"Okay then." Luis sighs.

"Time for your cheat sheets," Ms. Tremt replies, as she hands us each a flyer filled with facts about the fifties.

The president in 1951 was Harry S. Truman.

The Korean War was ongoing.

There were still farms in Brooklyn.

The Brooklyn Dodgers were as much a symbol of Brooklyn as the Brooklyn Bridge. (Do not say anything negative about the Dodgers. They are the pride of the borough!)

Popular musicians at the time were Nat King Cole, Tony Bennett, Patti Page, Frank Sinatra, and Bing Crosby.

The first color television program was broadcast on June 25, 1951, but color television sets were not available to the general public yet.

Popular TV shows were The Ed Sullivan Show, What's My Line?, You Bet Your Life, Howdy Doody, *and* The Lone Ranger.

"What about *I Love Lucy*?" Grace asks. "My grandfather loves that show!"

"Do *not*, under any circumstances, mention *I Love Lucy*," Ms. Tremt cautions us. "*I Love Lucy* premiered in October of 1951, so in July 1951 no one knew about it yet."

"Got it, Ms. Tremt!" Grace says with a salute.

"I hope you do—all of you," Ms. Tremt replies. "Time depends on it. The rest is just procedural. Very simple, if you pay attention."

"When I write the date down in this book, and your names, all three of you will immediately be transported there," the time-traveling librarian explains. "You will have three hours to complete your task. As you approach the three-hour mark, *The Book of Memories* will begin to glow. When that happens, you have exactly ten minutes left. That means ten minutes to write down the date you wish to return, find a safe place to set the book down, and let it grow so that you may step back into the present day. Do *not* lose track of time."

"And if we miss the three-hour mark completely?" I ask, a little afraid to hear the answer.

"Then I'll be stuck in 1951 with five bucks to my name forever?" Luis jokes.

"Exactly," Ms. Tremt replies seriously.

"Hey, I was kidding!" Luis protests.

"What about Plan B?" I ask. "You know, the one where you come rescue us if we're late?"

"There is no Plan B, Matt," Ms. Tremt says, looking into my eyes with a steely glare. "If you miss the cutoff, there is no return. There are risks to this adventure. I will not lie about that."

I'm all in, no matter what the risks are. I knew that from the second I realized I could change Grandpa Joe's life. But Grace and Luis? I'm not so sure it's worth it for them.

"We're going with you, Matt," Grace says as if she read my mind. "If you think you're traveling through time and changing history without us, you're crazy. Plus, I might get to try a real Brooklyn egg cream!"

"Ew, Grace," says Luis. "An egg cream? What is that?"

Ms. Tremt laughs. "It does sound pretty awful, Luis. But an egg cream is a sweet drink made with seltzer, chocolate syrup, and milk. It really is quite delicious."

"That sounds more my style," Luis says.

"Okay! C'mon, Matt. Let's do this!"

I grin at my friends. They really are the best. "Looks like we're all onboard, Ms. Tremt. 1951, here we come!"

"Excellent," Ms. Tremt says. "As long as you're all sure, and committed to the rules of the adventure . . . follow me."

We follow Ms. Tremt back to the empty classroom like ducklings heading for their first swim. Ms. Tremt opens *The Book of Memories*, takes the date card out of the little envelope on the first page, and removes the top from her fountain pen. Then she writes down all three of our names: *Matthew Vezza, Luis Ramirez, Grace Scott.*

Once again, the book sparkles and the words *Where would you like to go today?* appear in glowing green text.

Ms. Tremt checks her watch. "It's 3:15 p.m.," she says. "Please make sure your watches are wound, and read the same. You will need to complete your task and return to the present by 6:15 p.m. If you return on time, it will be 3:15 in the present, as if you had never left."

"Or be stuck in *Howdy Doody* land forever," Luis reminds us.

"*Howdy Doody* land?" I ask.

Luis shrugs. "*Howdy Doody* was a kids show in the fifties. My grandfather told me about it."

Ms. Tremt nods. "That's correct, Luis. And correct about making sure you do not miss your six fifteen deadline." She then turns her attention back to the book. Under the sentence *Where would you like to go today?* she writes the words *Bay Ridge, Brooklyn, New York. July 4, 1951.*

"Stand back," Ms. Tremt says.

"Um, Ms. Tremt," I try to interrupt, wanting to tell her that I have Uncle Alex's old street address, but it's too late.

The book begins to shake and stretch and grow until it takes up the wall again. When Ms. Tremt flips the cover open, a black-and-white image appears. It shows a bunch of teenagers sitting around a table.

"Hold hands, you three," Ms. Tremt instructs us. "It's time to go."

I grab Grace's right hand, and Luis grabs her

62

left. I wonder if he's squeezing her hand as tightly as I am.

"Now, walk slowly into the picture," Ms. Tremt says. "Stay calm and relax. Everything will be just fine if you remember the rules."

We hear Ms. Tremt's voice fading off as we take our first steps back in time.

"No modern-day references . . . no cell phones, no laptops, and no *I Love Lucy*," she calls from an ever-increasing distance. "And don't spend your whole five dollars in one place, Luis!"

Splat! I find myself sprawled out on top of something, with Luis on top of me, and Grace on top of him. Plus, we're all kind of groggy, like we just woke up from a deep sleep. Where are we? We all peek down, and realize we landed on top of an enormous refrigerator. We're in a kitchen— but not a family kitchen. A restaurant kitchen. Just as we're about to climb down, a waitress zips in on roller skates and peers in the fridge (while we all lean back and hold our breath). She grabs a bottle of ketchup and skates back out again. We all give a collective sigh of relief. When we're sure the coast is clear, we carefully get down. We're able to climb down from the top of the fridge to the sink and then to the floor. We stroll into the dining area of the restaurant and no one is the wiser.

So the good news is that with just a few steps, we've arrived safely in 1951. And we are most definitely in Brooklyn—you should hear the accents! *Dem Dodguhs are killin' me! Dese fries are drippin' in erl. Somebody get me a glass uh watuh.* I always thought Grandpa Joe and Uncle Alex were playing it up to make me laugh, but I guess it's really the way they talked back in the day.

Ms. Tremt did an excellent job with our wardrobe, and we fit right in with the crowd. *The Book of Memories* is now pocket-size, and it slips into the back pocket of my jeans.

But leave it to Grace to help us make a "Grace-less" entrance. (I can say that because I'm her friend.) "We're here! We're really here!" she squeals, rushing toward a booth without looking in front of her, and she nearly crashes right into a roller-skating waitress. "Watch where yer goin', honey," the waitress scolds as she zips on by. Her gum cracks loudly. We can't stop staring at her.

Grace finally takes a good look around. "Um, Matt . . . ," Grace says tentatively. "We're not . . ."

"At Uncle Alex's," I reply. "Yeah, I know."

I know we're supposed to limit our interactions, but someone's going to have to find out exactly where we are.

Grace, Luis, and I flop into an empty booth and try to act like we belong there. I slide my arm across the top of the seat and slouch down, trying to look cool and nonchalant.

"Matt," Grace says again.

"I *know*, Grace," I reply. "We have to figure out where we are, and how to get to Uncle Alex's. And you don't have to remind me that we don't have phones to pull up any maps, either. I know, I know!"

"Take it easy," Grace answers, a little annoyed. "I was going to ask if you thought it would be okay to order an egg cream. Since we're here and all. I'm dying to try one."

"Sorry, Grace, I'm stressing out a little," I admit. "That sounds like a good plan. Maybe our waitress will know how to get to Bay Vista Drive."

"Egg cream," Luis says, and gives a little shudder. "I'm sorry, I know Ms. Tremt told us they tasted good, but that name still grosses me out."

Our waitress rolls over and hands us three menus. I read the writing on the cover: MITCHELL'S DRIVE-IN.

Speaking of driving, the cars we see outside through the diner window are amazing. The engines are super loud, and it seems like the drivers have some kind of territorial ritual where they compete to see who can rev them louder. Some cars have flames on the sides, others are two-toned with colors that you don't see much on the road today—aqua blue and pink, yellow and mint green.

The drivers' outfits aren't as colorful as their cars. It seems like there is definitely an unspoken uniform requirement—rolled-up jeans, T-shirts, and slicked-back hair, just like Luis and me.

"Hi! I'm Margie, and I'll be serving you today," says the waitress, who's wearing a skirt, an apron, and a tiny hat that looks like a box on her head. "What can I get ya?"

"Three egg creams," Grace says.

"Oh man! I can't believe I'm actually going to drink something called an egg cream!" Luis moans.

Margie looks surprised. "You've never had an egg cream?"

"None of us have," I say. "And we're a little nervous."

Margie smiles. "You're all in for a treat! You want *chawclet*, vanilla, or black and white?"

"*Chawclet* sounds good," Luis says in his best Brooklyn accent. "And I'll take a *cheeseburguh* wit' fries."

"That five-dollar bill is really burning a hole in your pocket, Luis," Grace says with a chuckle.

"One more thing," I say to Margie. "Could you give us directions to Bay Vista Drive?"

It turns out Margie isn't from the neighborhood. And even the couple sitting next to us doesn't know exactly where Uncle Alex's street is.

"I'll ask those Ridgefield Prep kids over there," Margie tells us. "They gotta know. Money sticks with money, ya know."

It turns out, Margie is one smart cookie. Ridgefield Prep is the name of the prep school Grandpa Joe attended. The kids know exactly where Bay Vista Drive is—they're probably heading to Uncle Alex's party later too!

Ms. Tremt was right—the egg creams are actually pretty great. Even Luis thinks so. "It's like fizzy chocolate milk," he says. "Delish!"

And the roller-skating waitresses are pretty impressive. I don't even want to think what Grace would look like trying to balance a tray piled high with food while skating through tables. An epic disaster, I'm imagining.

I cough and tap my watch, and Luis gobbles up the last of his fries. Luckily it turns out that Bay Vista Drive is a short walk from Mitchell's, so we pay the bill—and give Margie a nice tip that makes her wink at us when we leave.

We have to move fast, but it's hard not to stop and gawk at the sights. It's cool and cloudy and misty, not at all what you'd expect from a July day, and everything looks kind of gray, especially in comparison to the colorful cars.

We walk past a Woolworth's five-and-dime

store, and it's clear that Luis could buy almost anything he needs there with his five dollars, from a pet parakeet to a complete cowboy costume.

Luis, though, has something other than shopping in mind. I see something rectangular and silver in his hand and he's pointing it down the street. It takes me a second to realize what he's doing . . . and then it hits me.

"LUIS, NO!" I shout. "No digital cameras allowed!"

Luis clicks the button and *poof*! He instantly disappears right in front of us.

"LUIS! Where did he go?" Grace wails. "What just happened?"

"He snuck a digital camera into 1951!" I yell. "What was he thinking?"

"WHERE IS HE?" Grace cries.

I have no idea. Ms. Tremt didn't warn us about this. Did Luis fly back to the present? Was he still here, somewhere in 1951? Or was he stuck in some spooky limbo in between? Could he be in a jail for people who break the rules of time travel? Who knows? But Ms. Tremt seemed really nervous about the rules. But there's no time to freak out. There's barely enough time to help Grandpa Joe. So I try to stay calm, cool, and collected.

"Look. We just have to believe that Luis will be back home waiting for us," I tell Grace. "Okay? Because there's nothing we can do right now."

"Okay," Grace agrees nervously. "But I'm not really okay with this."

"Neither am I, Grace," I reply. "But let's just keep moving."

It takes exactly eight minutes to walk from the drive-in to Uncle Alex's house. Eight minutes where wild and crazy thoughts of Luis being sucked into time warps rack my brain, but finally, we arrive.

"We're definitely in the nicer part of town," Grace notes as we gaze at the beautiful, and obviously pricey, homes on the street.

Bay Vista Drive is a quiet, hidden street. It seems like a secret place, and hardly like the busy avenues we just walked down.

It's easy to figure out which house is Uncle Alex's. Music is blasting from the backyard, and groups of teens are coming in and out.

"Let's slip in through the garage," I suggest as we head up the driveway. "It's probably empty, and then we can figure out our next steps before we mingle."

It's a good thing that we didn't start discussing our next plans out loud, because just then Uncle Alex slides out from underneath his Chevrolet Deluxe. It is a huge, beautiful car. I am relieved we haven't been talking about time travel. It would have been difficult to explain to him why were talking about getting back to the future in less than three hours, and stuff like that. So much for our private planning time.

"Oh hey, hello," Uncle Alex greets us, obviously surprised to see us as well. "Do I know you? What can I do for you?"

"I'm John's cousin, Matt," I say, making it up on the spot. "I think he told you we were coming. This is my friend Grace."

I figure Uncle Alex has got to know at least one John. I don't even know how that popped into my head, because honestly, I'm so stunned to see a teenage Uncle Alex that it's a wonder my brain can even process a single thought. If you think it's weird to travel more than sixty years into the past, imagine seeing someone you've only ever known as an old man suddenly appear right in front of you as a teenager. I can't stop staring.

"Sure, John from the golf team," Uncle Alex says, like he knows who I'm talking about. "I think I saw him by the pool earlier. I don't remember him mentioning that his little cousin was coming, but then again, there are a lot of people here I don't remember inviting, especially since it's not exactly beach weather today."

I nod. There's a brief moment of uncomfortable silence, so I try to break it. "Nice car," I say, sounding totally clueless.

"She's a beauty, all right," Uncle Alex says proudly. "I wanted to show it off to this girl I have my eye on, but for some reason it's not working right now. It's making me nuts!"

"Can I take a look?" Grace asks.

"Um . . . okay, I guess," Uncle Alex replies. He grabs a pair of overalls from a hook on the wall and tosses them to Grace. "Here. You can put these on. I don't want you to get your clothes dirty."

"Thanks!" Grace says as she puts them on over her '50s outfit.

Grace lies on the dolly and slides under the car, immediately banging her head in the process. "Oof!" we hear her say from under the car.

Uncle Alex looks at me, amused, and shrugs his shoulders. Grace doesn't inspire much confidence when she's fumbling around, but I know you can always trust her to know what she's doing.

"Her dad's a mechanic," I explain. "She's been crawling under cars since she could, well, crawl."

I know how Grace's mind works. She's in awe right now. It's a magnificent machine for sure, and I don't know anything about cars.

"She's a real beauty," Grace says as she rolls back out. "And if you have a wrench, I think I can fix your problem."

Uncle Alex digs through a toolbox and hands Grace a wrench. "Thanks," she says and rolls back under the car. Just a few short minutes later she rolls back out.

"The car should work now," Grace says. "It was just a loose valve cover gasket."

"I have to admit, I'm impressed," Uncle Alex says as he winks at Grace. "And I owe you one."

"I might hold you to that," Grace replies with a grin. "But I guess we'd better get to the party now. Maybe I'll see you later!"

Grace and I scurry through the garage's back door.

"Were you just flirting with Uncle Alex?" I ask Grace when we're finally alone. "Because that's kind of weird."

"No, I was not flirting, Matt." Grace laughs. "And I think *you're* weird for even thinking that."

"Guys, I know you're having fun and all, but the clock's still ticking," Luis interrupts.

"LUIS!" Grace screams. "What are you doing here?"

"What happened? Where did you go? Did you get stuck in some sort of time warp?" I ask.

"Nah, but I do have detention all next week," Luis explains. "Ms. Tremt pulled me out of here as soon as she saw my digital camera. I guess she can still see us from the present. She was really mad at me for breaking the time rules and all. I didn't know it would get me detention!"

"You're lucky that's all you got," Grace says as she gives Luis a big hug. "I'm so happy you're back. But what were you thinking?"

"I was thinking that I wasn't going to travel back in time and not get a picture!" Luis laughs. "Ms. Tremt, however, thought otherwise."

"So, since we're reunited and all, what's the plan now?" I wonder aloud.

"As much as I love being back together with you guys," Luis says, "I think we should split up to search for Grandpa Joe. Make the most of our time."

"Good idea," Grace says. "I'll take the kitchen. I need to wash the grease off my hands—and maybe I'll try making friends with some of the girls here."

Luis decides to mingle inside the house, while I agree to check out the backyard and pool area for signs of my grandfather.

I find a spot where I can scope out the scene without actually having to talk to anyone. There's a group of guys by the grill, cooking up hot dogs and talking sports. I get a little closer to them so I can listen to their conversation, in case they're Ridgefield Prep guys, and also to the game they've tuned into on a portable radio.

The talk is baseball. Brooklyn Dodgers baseball, to be exact. They're listening to the first game of a doubleheader between the New York Giants and the Brooklyn Dodgers, and the score is still double goose eggs. (That's 0–0 for you non-baseball-loving people.)

If Grandpa were outside, he would definitely be part of this crew. So I figure it's best to head inside and see if Grace and Luis have had any luck finding him.

"I found Patty Caravale," Grace whispers to me when I head to the kitchen. "She's pretty and she was floating around the room like a ballerina."

"Did she talk about Grandpa Joe?" I ask.

"She talked about Joe, and every other guy at the party," Grace says, rolling her eyes. "Who likes Joe, who does Joe like, who does Alex like, who likes Alex . . . it's like a Who's Who of crushes with the girls, but I still don't know where Grandpa Joe is! Oh, and by the way, hope you're not hungry! Check out this spread."

Before I mention the food, I have to tell you about the kitchen. It seems as if aqua might be the color of the time. I thought aqua cars were a little odd, but Grace and I are surrounded by a sea of aqua here—even the refrigerator is a bluish green! I'm starting to feel a little seasick, and it gets worse when Grace shows me the food that's been prepared.

Deviled eggs, tuna casserole, and the masterpiece of them all—a gigantic, wiggly green gelatin mold. The top is a darker green, and a little bit crusty, as if the gelatin mold had seen better days. And big chunks of something (I'm guessing fruit) are floating inside the jiggly mess. I put my hand to my mouth and gag.

"Truly gross," I say. "And definitely time to get out of here."

Grace picks up the gelatin mold and we head out of the kitchen.

"Would you like a slice?" Grace asks Luis sweetly when we find him in the living room.

"Of a slime experiment?" Luis grumbles.

"No, thank you. Are you trying to poison me or something? Get that green mess away from me!"

"You don't look happy, Luis." I chuckle. "What's going on?"

"Dude, this place is putting me to sleep. I can't believe how boring the conversations are. Who cares if your penny in your penny loafer is shiny or not?"

"No extreme athletes here?" I joke.

"Only extremely dull ones," Luis snaps. "Can we just find Grandpa Joe and get out of here already?"

That's exactly what I would like to do. But considering that none of us have even gotten a glimpse of my grandfather, I'm starting to have the heart-thudding, chest-tightening feeling of a panic attack.

"Everything okay?" a familiar voice asks from behind me.

It's Uncle Alex. If anyone knows where my grandpa is, it's him. I'm just going to have to go for it and ask, and hope it doesn't shift the course of the future too much.

"Oh yeah, we're great," I reply. "We're just

looking for that kid Joe. You know, the one who plays baseball for the Blue Angels? I heard he might get called up to the big leagues, and I thought I might get his autograph before he becomes a superstar."

"You mean my best friend, Joe," Uncle Alex says, laughing. "He's a superstar all right, but he's not here yet."

I try not to start hyperventilating.

"Why not?" I ask, attempting to sound a whole lot calmer than I feel.

"He's at that Giants-Dodgers doubleheader," Uncle Alex explains. "He promised he'll only stay for the first game so he won't miss the whole party. He should be here by six."

I know this might sound crazy, but the image of Grandpa Joe at Ebbets Field sends every panicked thought straight out of my body. I've read about Ebbets Field my entire life. People who love baseball talk about Ebbets Field like it's a sacred place. I've always wondered what it must have been like to see a baseball game there, for real. Now I'm going to get a chance.

"He's not getting here until six o'clock!" Luis

gasps as soon as Uncle Alex turns away to talk to a pretty girl.

"We're doomed," Grace moans.

"Ebbets Field," I whisper reverently. *"Ebbets Field.* I am so there!"

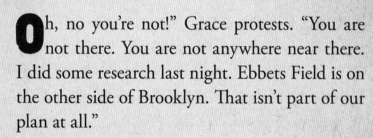

Oh, no you're not!" Grace protests. "You are not there. You are not anywhere near there. I did some research last night. Ebbets Field is on the other side of Brooklyn. That isn't part of our plan at all."

"Honestly, Matt, how are you going to get there and get back in time?" Luis adds.

"It's better than sitting here and just waiting," I reply. "Maybe I can persuade Grandpa to come back to the party early."

"Think about it, Matt," Luis says. "One,

you've got to get to a stadium you have no idea how to get to. Two, you have to find a teenage version of your grandfather inside this crowded stadium. Three, you need to somehow get him to agree to head back here with you, and oh yeah, one more little thing. Four, he has NO IDEA WHO YOU ARE!"

"You don't have to yell, Luis," I say. "I don't know how, but I'll find a way to make it work."

"Matt, please," Grace says softly. "We know he's coming here. If he gets here by six we have fifteen minutes to work with. I know it's not a lot of time, but we *know* he's coming. What if you don't get back in time? What if Luis and I are stuck here waiting for you while you have *The Book of Memories*?"

I take the book from my back pocket. This, at least, is an easy fix.

"You hold on to the book," I tell Grace as I hand her the book. "I am not giving up a chance to see Ebbets Field! Duke Snider. Roy Campanella. JACKIE ROBINSON! Not to mention the greatest sports fans to ever cram into a stadium. It's the stuff of legend. A field of dreams. Baseball is my life, Grace. If I don't get back in time, you can head home without me. I'll be fine here."

"Okay, still, even if that's what you want to do, will you consider that there's no way for you to actually do it?" Luis reminds me. "You've never been alone in a city; how are you going to do it in 1951? Think about it. You can't look up train schedules on the Internet. You can't grab a ticket to the game online. It's just impossible."

"I have to find a way," I reply. "I'll never forgive myself if I don't get there."

"Don't get where?" Uncle Alex interrupts.

I will admit that thinking that Uncle Alex may have heard even the teensiest bit of our conversation about life in the future sends my heart racing again. But I'm not ready to give up the dream yet.

"Ebbets Field," I tell him. "When you said that Joe was at the game, it reminded me that it's one thing I'd like to do before I go back."

"Go back where?" Uncle Alex asks.

"Um . . . Buffalo," I say, spying a painting of a herd of buffalo in the living room. "You know, we just came down for the fireworks, I don't know when we'll get down here again, and I'm not even sure if we'll get to see any fireworks in this mist."

"You know, I do owe your friend a favor," Uncle Alex says. "If she doesn't mind trading it in, I can give you a lift to the train station."

"That's one problem solved," Grace says. "But there's another one. A big one. How are you getting into the game, Matt?"

Alex winks as he takes a ticket out of his pocket.

"It must be your lucky day, kid," he says. "I was supposed to go with Joe, but you know, party and all. I'll go pull the car out front. Meet you outside."

I am aware that it is totally inappropriate to jump up and down with joy at this moment. Let me tell you, when I see that ticket, it takes every bit of willpower not to do just that.

"Matt, I'm just going to say this one more time," Grace says. "I don't think you should go. I don't want to even think about going home without you."

"I'd be fine, really." I laugh. "I could choke

down some tuna casserole if I had to to survive."

"Just get back here in time," Grace says seriously. "I'm not considering any other options."

Just then we hear the loud honk of Uncle Alex's Chevy.

"You coming, kid?" he calls as the three of us step onto the sidewalk.

"I'll see you before time's up," I whisper to Grace and Luis. "I promise. Relax. Enjoy some slime mold while I'm gone!"

I hop in the Chevy and look around for a seat belt, but there aren't any. Of course, I can't ask Uncle Alex about it, or I might mess up the persistence of time or something. I didn't realize how much more dangerous life was back in the '50s. So I hold on tightly while Uncle Alex takes me to the 86th Street station, where I can catch the 4th Avenue Line train. He gives me a wallop on the back and hands me his ticket and a couple of pennies (that was the train fare in 1951—two cents!).

"Enjoy, Matt," he says with smile. "See you back at the party later."

I start to get a little emotional. It's my uncle

Alex, after all. My grandpa's best friend in the world. And he's giving me the most awesome gift I could ever imagine getting. I think I might tear up if I don't get out of the car quickly.

Ha! Gotcha! I'm kidding. Everyone knows there's no crying in baseball!

"Thanks so much," I say as I close the car door behind me. "This is really like a dream come true."

"Glad I could make it happen," Uncle Alex says. "But if I hear you were cheering for the Giants . . . let me tell you, there will be some serious consequences to face when you come back to the party!"

"Never," I assure him. "Dodgers all the way!"

Now it's time to confess that I am a little nervous about entering the New York City subway system. You may have heard the rumors too. It's crowded. It's dirty. It's smelly. It's probably as gross as a slimy gelatin mold . . . well, maybe not that bad. Nothing could be that bad.

And it's not, really. It's actually pretty nice inside, a lot better than I expected. The ladies all look very dressed up, with swirling skirts and fancy hairstyles. (By that I mean all poofed up with a lot of hair spray—not like the simple straight or curly hairdos my mom's friends have.) A lot of the guys are dressed in suits—and from the snippets of conversation I hear, a couple are even heading to the baseball game.

I finally arrive at the stadium entrance at the corner of McKeever Place and Sullivan Place. I don't think I've ever really understood the word "breathless" before in my life, but that's exactly what I feel like as I gaze at the majestic stadium rising up from the streets of Brooklyn.

I step through an entrance and into the rotunda of Ebbets Field. I look up and see the lights of the chandeliers (at a baseball stadium!) are actually shaped like baseballs. I realize that I'm walking through history—baseball history. And just in case you're inclined to blow off the significance because it's "just baseball," let me remind you how the game changed a nation's history. I am stepping into the stadium of a team that literally changed the face of American sports forever. When Jackie Robinson signed with the Brooklyn Dodgers on April 15, 1947, he blasted through the color barrier the way his bat blasted through a baseball. As the first African-American player to play in the major leagues, he ended sixty years of segregation in pro ball.

So here I am, standing in this place, at this time. And all I can think is, *Thank you, Ms. Tremt. Thank you so very, very much.*

I take a deep breath, and it feels like the first one I've taken since I've left the subway station. I squeeze through the rowdy crowd to find my seat. Of course, in this perfect moment, I find my seat right next to the perfect person—my grandpa.

I stand at the end of the row so I can stare at him for a moment without him noticing me. It's one thing to sit on the couch and browse through old photos with your family. It's another thing entirely to find yourself face-to-face with the younger, stronger version of the man who's been one of the most meaningful influences in your life.

Young Grandpa Joe is handsome. And he's tall, tan, and muscular. He's a picture-perfect baseball player.

"He's an athlete," I whisper to myself. "A real athlete. In any time."

I'm still a little flustered by it all, but I know there's work to do, so I quietly make my way to the seat and sit there, just taking it all in, at least as much as I can.

Then I hear his voice, the voice I have heard every single day of my life. It jolts me out of my baseball dream state, because, while Grandpa Joe looks as if he could be a different person than the one I toss a ball to every morning, the tone of his voice sounds almost exactly the same—with a smidge more Brooklyn in it.

"Hey, buddy, I think you're in the wrong seat," Grandpa Joe says to me. "This seat belongs to my best friend."

"Yeah, your friend Alex," I say. "Hi. I'm Matt. I was just at Alex's party. He gave me the ticket since he wasn't going to make it himself. I've always wanted to see a game at Ebbets Field."

"Oh, okay. Hi, I'm Joe. Nice to meet you. So, whaddya think?" my teenage grandfather asks me as he points to the field.

"I think it's the most beautiful place on this Earth," I tell him honestly.

"I do too, kid," Grandpa Joe agrees. "Just don't tell the New York Giants I said that."

"Right! Alex told me you signed with them." I laugh. "And you might get called up soon."

"From your lips to the baseball gods' ears," Grandpa says. He turns away from me for a moment to look at the green baseball field. "It's all I've ever wanted."

Grandpa Joe fills me in on the game details. The Dodgers squeaked out a win in the first game. After being down 4–0, they came back to win 6–5 in the eleventh inning. Dodgers shortstop Pee Wee Reese and catcher Roy Campanella both hit home runs in a three-run eighth inning.

Now, in the second game of the doubleheader, Ralph Branca is on the pitcher's mound for the Dodgers. There are nearly 35,000 fans packed into the stadium, and I can hear every one of them. At the end of five innings, the game is tied 1–1.

"Another nail-biter," I observe.

"Yeah," Grandpa Joe says. "I hope the Dodgers score soon. I told Alex I would only stay to watch the first game. I definitely need to head back to the party after this next inning."

Well, that's a relief. If we leave after the sixth, we should make it back to Uncle Alex's with plenty of time to change the course of Grandpa's personal history.

"My friends are still at the party. Maybe we could go back together," I say hopefully.

"Sure, as long as you're not a Yankees fan." Grandpa Joe laughs.

"Never!" I smile. "My grandfather taught me better than that. Go, Dodgers!"

"I'd like to meet that fine man one day." Grandpa Joe chuckles, and I start to laugh too, but for a different reason. 1951 Grandpa would like to meet future Grandpa. That's some real time-travel humor!

"I'm sure you two would have a lot to talk about," I reply.

In the top of the sixth, Branca gets the

Giants out 1-2-3. He even gets Willie Mays to ground out.

"Say hey!" my grandpa says with a little laugh as Willie grounds out.

"Why do people call Willie Mays 'The Say Hey Kid'?" I ask.

Grandpa Joe tells me nobody knows for sure, but one story is it's because a reporter once heard Willie remark, "Say who, say what, say where, say hey!" After that the reporter referred to Willie as "The Say Hey Kid" and the nickname stuck.

The Dodgers bats come alive in the bottom of the inning. Campanella singles to left field. Cox shoots a single to right field in the following at bat, then the pitcher bunts them into scoring position. Grandpa Joe points out Hilda Chester, a fan who attends every game at Ebbets Field armed with a brass cowbell. She rings it furiously as Carl Furillo knocks a line drive that zips to right field, and Campanella then Cox stomp on home plate.

"Eatcha heart out, ya bums!" Chester calls to the Giants fans in the crowd.

The stadium is rocking with excitement, the

Dodgers are up 3–1, and I can't believe that it is actually time to get up and go, when Pee Wee Reese hits a fly ball to end the inning.

"Where you from again, kid?" Grandpa Joe asks as I start to rise from my seat.

"Buffalo," I lie.

"We should probably just stay till the end of the game," Grandpa says. "You can go to a pool party anytime. But you might never get a chance to see something like this again."

My heart skips a beat in my chest. We need to get back to the party, like, now!

"Oh, I never will see something like this again," I agree. "But it's okay, we should go. Alex really wanted you to get back to the party. And, um . . . some girl named Patty was asking about you too."

"Was she?" Grandpa Joe laughs. "Well . . . she can wait. Baseball's life, right, kid?"

"Um, right," I say, just sitting there sweating, trying to figure out what I can do to get Grandpa Joe out of there.

Tick. Tock. Tick. Tock.

I feel the seconds passing with each heartbeat.

"You look a little nervous," Grandpa Joe noticed. "Got a girl waiting for you back home?"

"Me? No, no girls waiting," I say. "Well, just one."

"What's her name?" Grandpa Joe asks.

"Mom," I lie. "I didn't tell my mom where I was going, and if she goes to pick me up at the party and finds out I'm here, she's going to kill me."

Grandpa Joe slaps my back, and I know he didn't mean to, but it hurts.

"You shoulda said something, kid." He laughs. "Whaddya waitin' for? Let's get outta here!"

Of course, no real fan would ever leave a game before the last out, and the diehard fans at Ebbets Field let us know just what they think about us, booing and hissing as we exit the stadium.

Back on the train, I grill Grandpa Joe about his life.

"How do you like Ridgefield Prep?"

"Is it tough hanging around all those rich kids all the time?"

"Do you ever eat at Mitchell's Drive-In?"

"Are you going to ask Patty out on a date?"

"What will you be thinking when you step up to the plate for the first time as a New York Giant?"

"You should be a reporter, kid." Grandpa Joe laughs. "Always with the questions."

There's just one question on my curious mind now, though. Can I stop Grandpa from dancing with Patty so he can finally get his shot at the big leagues?

By the time we get back to the party, Grandpa Joe seems especially eager to see his buddies, and maybe a little eager to get away from me. I'm not hurt—I know I must seem like a strange, pesky kid to him here.

"Traitor!" one guy jokingly calls to Grandpa from his lounge chair. "Get your Giant butt out of here!"

"Aw, come on, you know I'll always bleed Dodgers blue, John," Grandpa yells back. "No matter what team I play for."

Mental note: The guy by the pool could be my "cousin" John—the relative I made up so Uncle Alex would let us into the party. I need to stay away from him at all costs.

I head back inside and run smack into Uncle Alex on the way to the bathroom.

"Was it worth the trip?" he asks.

"Was it ever!" I gush. "Thanks again!"

Grace spies me from the kitchen, and I can see her shoulders drop immediately as the stress leaves her body.

"Matt!" she says. "Get over here. Now!"

"Sure thing, sergeant," I tease her.

The hug I get from Grace is a pretty special thing. It's like all the years of our friendship mixed up with a couple of heapings of worry and relief wrapped in a clumsy, but comforting, embrace.

"I'm sorry if I scared you," I say to her.

"It's okay," Grace answers. "Just promise that you will NEVER DO IT AGAIN!"

"Pinky promise," I reply, holding out my little finger.

We lock pinkies and pull, just as Luis walks in.

"Hey, I want a piece of that pinky action," he says, holding out his finger. "What are we promising, anyway?"

"That we will find another friend to take your place as soon as we get home," Grace says. "Kidding!"

Outside the window, we can hear someone yell, "I can't believe you'll be playing with those guys in a couple of months! Willie Mays, Joe! You're gonna be playing baseball with WILLIE MAYS!"

Grace looks outside and blinks her eyes in disbelief.

"Whoa. Grandpa Joe is really good-looking," she says.

"Come on, Grace, don't say that," I complain, giving her a friendly shove. "It just sounds all kinds of wrong."

Grace looks embarrassed for a minute, until she sees that Luis and I are cracking up. Then she joins in.

"Sounds like a fun time in here," Grandpa says from the doorway. "These your friends, kid?"

"My best friends, Joe," I reply. "This is Grace,

and this is Luis. Grace, Luis, this is soon-to-be-a-famous-baseball-player Joe."

"I like the sound of that," Grandpa says with a grin. "It's nice to meet you, Grace and Luis."

"Would you like a slice?" Grace says, as she holds up the disgusting green gelatin mold, which looks like it hasn't been touched by anyone at the party.

"Not a chance." Grandpa Joe laughs. "You're not getting that poison into me."

He pulls us into a huddle to tell us a secret.

"I don't think anyone has ever eaten it," he whispers. "Personally, I think Patty has just been bringing that same mold from party to party for the past year!"

We're all laughing so hard Luis starts to snort, when suddenly loud music fills the air. A girl in a poodle skirt—almost identical to the one Ms. Tremt wanted Grace to wear—rushes through the kitchen and pulls me by the hand.

"It's mambo time!" she shouts. "Come on, everybody!"

Warning: The next part of the story is absolutely terrifying. The poodle-skirt girl drags me to the backyard, where a crowd of teenagers are wiggling this complicated-looking dance move with lots of footwork, and she expects *me* to do it too!

"The mambo started in Cuba," poodle-skirt girl informs me. "You just have to feel the music."

I watch as the girl holds her arms out at her side and waves them to the beat and wiggles her hips. I try to copy her movements, but I'm afraid that I look more like a sick chicken than a suave dancer.

Misery loves company, and I am thrilled to see Grace and Luis standing in the backyard pretending that they know how to mambo too. Three sick chickens in this coop, that's for sure.

From the corner of my eye, I see Grace doing this incredibly awkward flapping motion with her arms. She's actually smacking a few dancers in the head, so there's some room opening up around her, and that's when I see that she's trying to gesture to me and Luis to tell us to look her way.

Finally, I see what Grace is making all the fuss about. Grandpa Joe is talking to Patty near the steps of the pool! He's mamboing pretty smoothly, I have to say. I guess the dancing gene didn't get passed down to me.

Grace continues to bump into and trip over people as she mambos her way over to my side.

"What's the plaaaan, Matt?" she sings along to the music.

"I don't knooooow, Grace," I sing back. "We just need to get Grandpa Joe away from the pool steps, right? How hard can that be? He's a really nice guy. I'll just say, 'Joe, I need to talk to you for a minute,' and I'll lead him away from the pool. Then he can dance with Patty. Just not near the pool."

"Got it," Grace says, as I spin her away from me with a laugh.

She bumps and trips her way back over to Luis.

"So, here's the deal," I hear her begin to sing.

A minute later Grace is spinning back my way. I'm starting to get a little worried that Grace might get kicked out for being a party crasher, literally. She's inflicting a lot of bruises, crashing into people with her manic mambo moves.

"Luis says your plan is too shaky," Grace sings to me. "We need something totally foolproof."

"Well, does he have any better ideas?" I ask, then I spin her back to Luis.

Grace is like a whirling, twirling knockout weapon on the dance floor at this point, and when the record starts to skip, Grace tries to keep dancing to it and looks like a weird dancing robot.

"He doesn't," she says as she spins back to me.

"Well, neither do I," I reply as I spin her back.

"Enough," Grace says the next time she spins back to me. "I'm getting dizzy. I'll figure it out myself."

I'm feeling a little annoyed, so I put a little muscle into Grace's next spin. I close my eyes and grimace when I see her hurtling toward Grandpa Joe and Patty. *Bonk!* Grace crashes into the pair and falls down. Hard.

"I'm so sorry," Grace apologizes from her spot on the floor at their feet. "I'm not much of a dancer."

"Looks like someone could use some lessons." Grandpa Joe laughs. "What do you say, Patty?"

"Anytime!" Patty replies.

"How about right now?" Grace asks, a little

too anxiously. Grandpa Joe and Patty are even closer to the edge of the pool.

"Well, anytime except right this minute," Patty says with a laugh, batting her eyelashes at Grandpa Joe. "I'm having too much fun right now."

I watch as Grace slinks away from them. I'm worried that she's embarrassed, but then I notice that when Grace turns the corner, she starts to smile. I know that look. Grace has an idea. She knows just what she's going to do now.

I just have to hope that it will all happen in due time.

I can tell we've reached the time to hit it out of the ballpark when I hear Aunt Patty squeal, "'Ballerina'! I *love* this song!"

I panic when I see Grandpa Joe hold out his hand to Aunt Patty.

"May I have this dance?" he asks her.

I don't know what Grace has planned, but I don't think I have time to sit around and find out. I wiggle my way over to the dancing duo. But just as I'm close, Luis gets to Grandpa Joe before me.

"Hey, Joe. Hey, Patty," he says. "I think you're dancing a little close to the edge of the pool. So why don't you guys mambo your way over?" he asks, doing a funny little dance move, and starts to drag Patty away from the pool and lead her over to a grassy area by her elbow.

I'm so shocked I can't believe it. Of course! Just tell them, hey, you're dancing a little too close to the pool's edge. I shake my head and smile in relief. We did all that agonizing about getting Patty and Joe away from the pool for nothing.

But I'm celebrating too soon. Patty refuses to move. "I can't dance on the grass," she says. "Look, I have heels on. They'll sink in the grass and mud. I need to stay here on the concrete." She looks up at Grandpa Joe and smiles. "And I feel safe with Joe! If I start to slip, you'll catch me, won't you?"

Joe puts his arm around Patty's waist and smiles. "Of course!" he says. "I wouldn't let anything happen to you!"

Luis turns to me and shrugs as if to say, *I tried.* So it's up to me. I walk over to Joe and tap him on the shoulder.

"Hey, Joe, sorry to bother you," I babble as I hold his arm and pull him away from Patty so he can't move away from me. "Can I talk to you for a minute? It's important."

Grandpa Joe turns toward me and grins politely, but I can see that he's not feeling as polite as his smile seems.

"Any other time, kid, but not right now, okay?" he says. "I think it's apparent that I'm a little tied up at the moment. You see, there's a beautiful girl here who wants to dance. And I want to dance with her. So you're going to have to wait."

I can't let it go. Just one small chance—that's all I have.

"Um, Joe? This . . . this . . . it just really c-c-can't wait . . . ," I stammer.

Grandpa looks concerned for a minute, and that's when I make my big mistake. I relax. When I do that, he can sense that it's probably not the emergency I'm making it out to be. And then, out of the corner of his eye, he sees my "cousin" John start to move in on Patty.

"Look, kid, I'll be right with you, okay?" he

says, sounding totally annoyed now. "Just *after* this dance!"

Grandpa Joe moves back away from me and puts an arm around Aunt Patty's waist.

"Sorry, she promised this one to me," he tells John. "C'mon, Patty."

No! No! No! No! No! I scream inside my head as they start to dance. Luis and I watch helplessly. Joe is staring at Patty with a huge grin on his face as they dance, totally oblivious to the fact that his foot is right on the pool's edge. *It's going to happen any second now,* I think miserably. *This entire trip back in time has been a total waste.*

"JOOOOOOE!" Grace screams as she stumbles across the backyard waving her arms frantically toward Grandpa and Aunt Patty. "Don't dance with her! Dance with *me*! I . . . I . . . I LOVE YOU!"

Luis and I are frozen in place. We're totally in shock. The rest of the crowd starts to buzz with chatter. They're shocked too, but they're also pointing and laughing. I guess it's because Grace is the girl who just bumbled her way across the mambo floor.

I try to wrap my head around it.

Shy Grace. Quiet Grace. Stay-behind-the-scenes Grace. That girl, she's our BFF. This girl? I've never seen her before in my life.

Grace has to be aware that every single person at the party is now staring at her and thinking, *What's up with the wacky kid?*

But, magically . . . incredibly . . . somehow . . . it works.

Grandpa stops dancing, says something in Aunt Patty's ear, and disentangles himself from her. Then he walks over to Grace and looks her in the eye.

"Are you okay, kid?" he asks, concerned.

Grace just stands there and stares back at him, until the last notes of the song drift through the air. And then, when the moment of danger has passed, Grace shrugs her shoulders.

"Ha-ha-ha! I was kidding, daddy-o," she says with a chuckle. "You're not really my type."

I look at Luis and we both mouth the same thing to each other: *Daddy-o?* What book did Grace pull that one out of?

Now that the goofy-girl show is over, the

partygoers make their way back to their regularly scheduled activities—pairing up for slow dances, doing cannonballs into the pool, and talking about the Brooklyn Dodgers, of course.

"Dodgers have a six-game lead for first place after that doubleheader today," someone reports to Grandpa Joe.

"Looks like the Giants really need you," I add.

"I just hope I get a chance to help," Grandpa Joe says humbly.

"I think you will," Luis says slyly. "I just have a feeling about these things."

Grandpa Joe and Grace stare at each other for a moment. Then Grace laughs weakly and lightly punches Grandpa Joe on the arm.

"Where's your girl?" she asks. "There's something I've been meaning to tell her."

Grandpa Joe points Grace in Patty's direction. Luis and I follow her. We can't wait to hear what she has to say.

"I'm really sorry I interrupted your dance," Grace apologizes. "I think I'm light-headed because I haven't eaten anything yet. And I am definitely going to have to take you up on those dance lessons one of these days."

"That's okay, sweetie," she says. "I understand." Patty laughs. "Joe is hot stuff!"

Patty has never been one to hold grudges, it seems.

"That's for sure." Grace smiles as she glances my way. "Just do me one little favor."

"Sure thing," Patty replies. "What is it?"

"Promise me that if you dance with him again, you'll dance over here, away from the pool. And I know you don't want to dance on the grass, but there's another big patch of cement here leading into the house. And look, there's a lot more room for you to be all whirly and twirly and, you know, ballerina-like."

"Oooh! I like the way you think," Patty says.

I stare in wonder and admiration at my friend Grace. Grace—the kid who always shared her crayons with me in kindergarten. Grace—the only kid who didn't laugh at me for eating paste because it looked just like a can of white frosting. Grace—who, when Ms. Tremt said time travel was powered by positive energy, went above and beyond the call of duty to make sure Grandpa

Joe got his chance to be a Major League Baseball player.

"I like the way you think too, Grace," I say, and we smile at each other. But there's no time to lose. Because *The Book of Memories* is starting to glow. We have exactly ten minutes to get back home.

Grace, Luis, and I head inside and find a small, empty room off the kitchen where we can celebrate our victory. All signs point to Grandpa Joe leaving the party with his ankle in one piece! I can't even believe it.

"This might call for a victory dance," Luis says, and laughs.

"Okay, anything but the mambo," I tease Grace. "I'd like to get back home in one piece. Ready to go, Grace?"

Something's not right though. Grace has that

look again. Well, not *the* Look, but a different Grace look—the one where you can tell that Grace is realizing something. Realizing that something is wrong.

"Wait!" she says. "Wait . . . wait . . . WAIT!"

"We're waiting, Grace," Luis says. "Do you mind telling us what we're waiting for?"

"Yes. I mean, no. I mean, I don't mind. It's just that—think back, guys. Remember when we were talking to Matt's grandparents at dinner the night before we traveled back in time?"

"We remember," Luis and I reply in unison.

"Grandpa Joe said that your great aunt Patty brought her sister Jeanie to visit him after he had the accident."

"Oh no!" I gasp. "He said even though it ended his baseball career, something wonderful came out of that July Fourth. Grandma Jeanie! What if he never meets Jeanie?"

"What did we do?" Luis moans. "Are we going to get in trouble for breaking the rules of time? Do you think Ms. Tremt is going to give us detention?"

"Luis, think!" I say, shaking his shoulders.

"Detention is the *least* of our worries!"

"Because if there's no reason for Patty and Jeanie to visit Grandpa Joe . . . ," Grace starts to explain.

"Then there's no Grandma Jeanie!" I wail, smacking my head. "And no Mom. And no ME!"

"Relax, Matt," Grace says.

I growl back at her.

"I know, you hate when people say that to you," Grace says. "Sorry, but we really need to stay calm so we can think this through. We don't have much time left."

"Maybe Jeanie is here at the party?" Luis suggests.

"And how do we think we're going to find out?" I snap at him. "Do we just yell out, 'Hey, Jeanie!' and see if anyone answers?"

"That's an idea!" Luis says.

"Luis, I was being sarcastic," I inform him. "As I was just saying . . ."

"No time for 'just saying,'" Luis says.

A moment later he yells, "HEY, JEEEEANIE!" through the house.

"Well, that was a great idea," I say snarkily.

"Now we know that she's not here. How are we going to find out where she actually is?"

"We're doomed," Grace cries. "Totally, epically doomed."

"Enough," I groan. "I can't think while you're talking."

"I don't know what you're so busy thinking about," a girl suddenly interrupts me. "And I'm very sorry to disturb you by talking, but . . . were you looking for me?" she asks Luis.

"Jeanie?" Luis asks.

"Yes, that's my name," she answers. "The one you were just screaming."

Luis is too relieved to be embarrassed. We all are.

"Yeah, I'm sorry about that, but . . . would you happen to be Patty's little sister?" he asks.

"Yeah, what's it to you?" Jeanie asks.

"JOOOOOOOOOOOOOOE!" Luis yells.

"JOOOOOOOOOOOOOOOOOOE!" Grace cries.

"JOOOOOOOOOOOOOOOOOOOOOOE!" I scream at the top of my lungs.

Jeanie is looking at us like she may have to

call someone to remove us from the premises, when Grandpa appears.

"You know, for three little kids, you guys are awfully loud," he says.

"The louder the better," I say. "Just like Hilda Chester."

"You three may be even louder than Hilda." Joe laughs.

Luis quickly makes the introduction that my future is depending on.

"Joe, Jeanie. Jeanie, Joe," he says.

Remember how Grandpa Joe said it was love at first sight? He wasn't kidding. Even *I* almost saw fireworks.

"Jeanie . . . hi. May I ask you for this dance?" he says tentatively, and not sounding like the cool, assured athlete he acted like when he was with Patty.

"You may," Jeanie replies, her eyes shining. "And I will say yes."

Grandpa holds out his hand and Jeanie places hers into his. Seriously, there aren't hearts and violins, but there may as well be. It is a magical moment.

"Well, my work here is done," Luis notes.

"It sure looks that way," Grace agrees. "What do you say we . . ."

Grace is suddenly interrupted by a forceful tap on her shoulder.

"I was having so much fun," a tearful Patty cries. "Why did you three have to interfere?"

Looks like it's damage-control time—and the control had better be fast! But then Patty laughs.

"I'm just teasing you guys. Just between the four of us, I've always thought John was cuter than Joe anyway."

Just then Jeanie comes over—just for a moment—to tease her sister. "Tough luck, Patty," she says. "He's all mine now!" And we all laugh, even Patty.

Then another one of Patty's friends comes by with the legendary gelatin mold.

"Patty, what do you want to do with this?" she asks. She looks at the three of us. "You guys look hungry. Would you like some?"

"Gee, I'm stuffed," I lie.

"I'm allergic to gelatin," Grace fibs.

"You know, it looks interesting, and I'm sure

you're an amazing cook, but I'm just not an adventurous eater," Luis admits.

"No problem. It will keep," Patty says as she puts the wiggly mess back in the fridge.

It's a good thing she doesn't see the gagging and puke faces we all make as Aunt Patty, Grandma Jeanie, and her friend leave the room.

"One thing I won't miss about 1951 is the food. Except maybe the egg creams! Who would have thought it?" Luis jokes and checks his watch. He gasps. "Dude, it's time to go!"

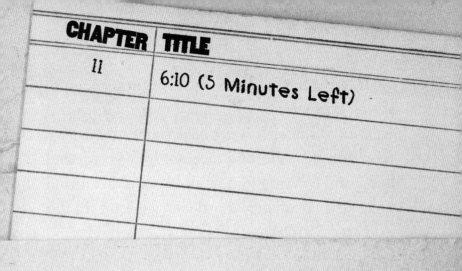

Okay, we have exactly five minutes left. We'd better say good-bye fast," Grace advises. "Remember, we still have to find a place for the book to expand so we can get back home."

"I don't think we'll have to look far," Luis says, as he points to Uncle Alex slow dancing with a girl. "I think the garage should be empty for a bit."

"You're full of ideas today," I tease Luis. "And that's the best one you've had."

It's time for the hardest part of the adventure: saying good-bye to Grandpa. I mean, I know I'll see him again when I get back home. But I have to admit, it would be supercool to have a friend like him to hang out with. I wouldn't mind hanging around 1951 a little longer, even if I did have to eat tuna casserole. But rules are rules. So the three of us walk over to him to say good-bye.

"Joe, I just wanted to thank you again before I leave," I say as I shake his strong hand. "And good luck in the show."

"Heading back to Buffalo?" Joe asks.

"Something like that," I reply. "I've got a long trip ahead of me, so I don't have a lot of time to chat. It was great watching the game with you, and I'm sorry I asked you so many questions on the ride home."

"Not at all, kid," he says. "It was a great day. A really great day."

I start to walk away when Grandpa yells, "Catch!"

I've heard that command so many times my body instinctively turns toward him, and I cradle the ball in my hand. I have to admit, it stings—a

122

lot. Teenage Grandpa has got an arm!

I roll the ball around in my hand and see that there is writing on it.

The ball is signed—by Willie Mays! I rub my eyes to make sure I'm seeing things clearly, and hope there aren't any rules about bringing it back with me.

"Just a little something to take back to Buffalo with you," Joe says. "Hopefully Willie won't mind giving me another one when I'm playing on his team."

Then Grandpa Joe turns to Grace.

"Kid!" he says as he ruffles his hand through her hair. "You'd better call Patty for those dancing lessons the next time you're in town."

"Sure thing," Grace says.

"So long, Joe," Luis says. "I'll cheer for you when you're pitching for the Giants. Good luck!"

"Thanks, Luis," Grandpa says. "Definitely come out to the games and cheer me on. All three of you! I'll need all the support I can get. Don't forget me," Grandpa says.

"Oh, we won't!" all three of us say at the same time.

We race to the garage and I pull *The Book of Memories* from my pocket. At the same time, I unluckily slip on a patch of oil and the book goes flying into the air. Amazingly, Luis makes the greatest catch of his life and scoops it up before it hits the floor.

"You need to write down the date," Grace says hurriedly. "On 'due date'—the card—like Ms. Tremt did."

She hands Luis a pen.

"Okay!" Luis says as he frantically scribbles a date on the card.

Luis opens the book and puts up against the wall. We watch silently as it expands and fills the garage wall.

We all hold hands and walk into the picture. "Good-bye, 1951. Hello, 1916!" Luis practically sings out.

Suddenly I realize what Luis actually just said.

"W . . . W . . . WHAT DID YOU JUST SAY?" I ask, not really wanting to know the answer to that question. "And please don't tell me that's what you wrote down in *The Book of Memories*!"

But it's too late. The image that we walked into is Washington Avenue—in 1916! It's not an avenue at all—it's a dirt road with farmland on either side. Sands Middle School doesn't even exist!

"Oh man, I'm sorry, sorry, sorry!" Luis apologizes as he steps away from a cow. "I had 1951 in my head—and the '19' just slipped out!"

"Look out!" Grace warns, just in time for us to jump out of the way of a horse-drawn ice truck.

There weren't any people around when we stepped through, but there may be soon.

"This could get bad . . . fast," Luis whispers.

"I think it already did," Grace moans.

"Guys, I could have dealt with being stuck in 1951, I really could. But 1916? What are we going to do?" I ask. My stomach is churning. I think I'm going to be sick.

Suddenly, infuriatingly, Luis *smiles*!

"Luis, how can you possibly smile at a time like this?!" I yell.

"Because I know how we're going to get back," he says. "Remember how my camera made Ms. Tremt zap me back to the present? We just have to flash around that 1951 money she gave us. We're in 1916, remember? That money is from the future, and can't exist here."

We all frantically dig into our pockets. Luis is first. He pulls out a quarter. "Hey look," she yells to a passerby. "This quarter is dated 1950—"

Poof! Luis is gone!

A couple turns to look at Grace. And before she even shows them a coin, *poof!* She's gone.

It's my turn. And it better work just as quickly for me, because by now a small crowd has gathered.

"Hi, guys," I say. "Did you ever see a dollar bill from 1949? No? Would you like to—"

Poof! I look around. Grace, Luis, and I are all on the floor in the Sands Middle School library, surrounded by whispering students and boxes of Ms. Tremt's books—just the way it was when we left.

Ms. Tremt quickly helps us all to our feet.

"Well done, Grace, Luis, and Matt," Ms. Tremt says, for the benefit of the bewildered kids in the library. "That is a fabulous magic trick. A very exciting entrance indeed! We'll need to work on it a bit more, but your costumes are perfect for your school project, Fashions Through the Times. Well done!"

A few kids giggle as Ms. Tremt escorts us to the back room.

"How did you get back home without showing a coin?" I ask Grace.

"It was her saddle shoes," Ms. Tremt explains. "They didn't exist in 1916, so the minute people saw them, she bounced back home."

"Ms. Tremt, you're not going to believe what happened to us!" Grace gushes. "We didn't even land at the party, and we had to find our way there, and we saw the most amazing things, and . . ."

Luis and Grace fill Ms. Tremt in on all the details, but I stay quiet. For some reason, I have a strange feeling Ms. Tremt somehow, some way, already knows all about our adventure. But how could she? I guess that's another mystery we'll have to solve one day.

I reach into my pocket—I decide I want to show Ms. Tremt my baseball autographed by Willie Mays after all. But when I put my hand in my pocket, all I feel is loose change. The ball is gone! A wave of sadness washes over me—and then a wave of worry. What else didn't make it into the present?

"Ms. Tremt, did our adventure work? Did Grandpa Joe become a pitcher for the New York Giants?" I ask.

"Matthew, in due time you'll find the answers to all your questions," she says gravely. But I could swear her lips start to curve just the slightest bit into a smile. "But right now I need you to hand over *The Book of Memories*, please."

I sigh as I hand the book over. I wonder where it will travel next.

I may not know *where*, but I don't have to wait long to find out with who. As soon as I give Ms. Tremt *The Book of Memories*, she turns right around and says, "Jada? Here's the book we discussed."

Jada Reese is in my English class. I notice she's wearing a very furry, very Ms. Tremt–like scarf as she takes the book. She and Ms. Tremt exchange a knowing glance. Then Jada smiles at me and says, "Hi, Matt! Did you have a nice trip?"

I just nod silently as I think, *Jada, you have no idea.*

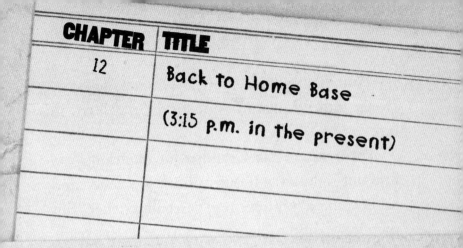

As soon as school is over, all three of race back to my house. I throw my backpack on the floor and give Grandpa the biggest hug ever.

"Did you get detention or something?" Grandpa Joe asks, half joking, half not.

"Nope," I say. "But Luis did. All week!"

"What did you do now?" Grandpa Joe asks Luis with a laugh.

"I just broke one of the rules about electronic devices," Luis explains with a shrug.

"You kids will never learn," Grandpa Joe says. "Keep those things in your locker and learn to talk to one another!"

I'm dying to ask Grandpa Joe questions—to find out right away if our mission succeeded and he became a professional baseball pitcher. But there's no time right now; it's time to get ready for my next big game.

I give Grandpa Joe another hug just because. Now Grandpa starts to get a little suspicious. He touches my forehead with the back of his hand.

"You're feeling a little warm, Matt," he says. "You'd better get Grandma to take your temperature. Can't risk getting sick before play-offs. Do you want to lie down for a little while?"

"I'm fine, Grandpa, really," I say.

So, it seems, is Grandpa. Better than ever, in fact. The limp, for instance. It's gone.

Luis and Grace invite themselves over for dinner after my game that afternoon. They both have noticed that Grandpa Joe isn't limping anymore.

"I can't believe it," Grace says hopefully. "Could we have really changed his life?"

130

"I think so," Luis says. "He seems, I don't know, happier."

I know that Grace and Luis will probably think I'm being corny, but I can't *not* say what I want to say now.

"You guys are really the *best* best friends," I say gratefully. "I would never have had enough positive energy to do this alone. It took teamwork, and I had the greatest team ever."

"Next to the Brooklyn Dodgers." Luis laughs.

Grandpa is not so happy that he forgets to come over and give his pregame speech, though.

"Matt, I know I've said this a million times—" he starts to lecture.

"A million and two," I correct him.

"Okay, funny guy," he says. "It's time to get serious. You know how to do this, Matt. I'm not sure why you let your nerves get to you when you're standing on the mound, because I know that you know how to do this. You've learned from the best."

"It might be Nick Falcone making me nervous," I suggest. "You know Nick Falcone. The hulking giant with the monster swing."

131

"Matt, I taught you better than that." Grandpa Joe sighs. "Once you believe someone is better than you, you're already defeated. Baseball is a game for thinkers. Think about everything I've taught you. It's all you need to blow the ball right by Nick Falcone, or any other batter."

I know Grandpa is right. I always know he's right. But there's just a switch that flips on when I step onto the mound. A switch that blocks out all the things I *should* know, and fills my mind with worries and other things.

Except today that switch seems to be broken. When I step onto the mound, I can only hear Grandpa's voice.

Your shoulder's open. Check yourself. Check your feet. Balance, kiddo.

I run through the checklist before every pitch, and it works! After Nick Falcone fouls off two pitches, I set my mind, and my fingers, on my cutter.

He's going to fall for it, I tell myself.

When I see the catcher sign for the cutter, I know he believes it too.

I hope I don't sound like I'm bragging, but I really wish you could see this pitch. It heads perfectly for the strike zone, then drops like a yo-yo on a string, right under Nick Falcone's bat.

"Strike three!" the ump yells with gusto.

My team wins 6–0. It isn't even close.

"Who's on your side, Matt?" I hear Grandpa cheer from the bleachers.

You are, Grandpa, I tell myself. *You always are. You're the best.*

Back at home, I can smell the chicken cutlets Grandma Jeanie is frying. They smell like home, and infinitely better than tuna casserole.

"Just a minute, guys," I tell Grace and Luis. "I have to wash up and change out of my uniform."

I go to my room to grab some fresh clothes to put on. I open one of my drawers and get the shock of my life. It's *there.* The Willie Mays autographed ball! This day just keeps getting better and better.

Grandpa can't stop talking about my game over dinner. It's actually a little embarrassing. But just a little.

"Jeanie, I wish you had been there to see him," he says. "He reminded me of myself back in the day."

"Then I know just what he looked like, Joe." She laughs. "Remember, I never missed one of your games after we started dating."

"I remember," Grandpa Joe says. "I always looked to the stands to see where you were. It helped me relax."

"Heck of a game, Matt," Grandpa Joe continues. "And I'm glad you invited your friends over tonight. I found something today that I wanted to share with the three of you. Be right back."

Grandpa heads upstairs, and Grandma goes back to the kitchen to check on dessert.

When we have a minute alone, the questions start to fly.

"Did you ask him if he played for the Giants?" Luis asks.

"Does he remember us from the Fourth of July party?" Grace wonders.

"Relax!" I tell them. "There's time to find out the answers. I don't want him to get suspicious."

Grandpa comes back to the table with an old, tattered shoe box.

"I can't believe I found this today," he says. "I've been looking for this shoe box for years." He turns his head toward the kitchen and calls for my grandma.

My grandfather gently removes the lid from the box and hands it to Grandma.

"Joe, let me clear off the table first," she says. "You don't want to mess that stuff up."

Luis, Grace, and I hop up to help Grandma. When the table is cleared, we huddle around Grandpa.

"Check these out," he says proudly.

He pulls out a stack of old black-and-white photos and places them on the table. I see the photo on top, and I want to gasp, I really do. I can tell Luis and Grace are holding their breath too. I feel like my heart is about to burst.

The photo shows Grandpa, dressed in a gray uniform. The words "New York" are embroidered on the front of the shirt. It's a New York Giants away uniform, and Grandpa is standing on the pitcher's mound at Ebbets Field.

He made it to the major leagues after all!

"Look at this one," Grandpa Joe says as he pulls out a photo of him and Willie Mays, arm in arm, celebrating the 1951 National League pennant win.

"Can you tell us the story of the Shot Heard 'Round the World?" I ask.

"Aw, come on, Matt, you must have heard that one a million times," Grandpa Joe says.

"A million and two." I laugh. "But it always seems like it's the first time."

"It was the ninth inning," Grandpa Joe begins. "The Giants were home for game three of the pennant, the decisive game. We were losing to the Dodgers, 4–2."

"And you were torn, because you were a Dodgers fan, right?" Grace says.

"Are you kidding, Grace?" Grandpa Joe laughs. "I was called up to the majors in September. I was a Giant now! I wanted to beat those bums. I wanted to win! Anyway, no one thought we'd ever win against the Dodgers. We'd already beat the odds by winning the last seven games of the regular season to tie them.

Everyone figured we had used up all our winning chips. But we hadn't. We won the first game, but we lost game two to the Dodgers, 10–0. That set the stage for the third game at our home field, the Polo Grounds. Back then the National League pennant was decided by whoever won two games out of a three-game series. Nowadays it's a lot longer—it's best four out of seven games.

"Then it was the ninth inning. Our last chance to score and win the game. Our shortstop, Alvin Dark, started the ninth inning rally. And our third baseman, Bobby Thomson, finished it. Ralph Branca came in to pitch for the Dodgers against Thomson. There were two men on base. Bobby watched a strike go back on the inside corner for his first pitch. But the second pitch—a fastball up and in—well, he just smoked that ball down the left field line! It disappeared into the lower deck stands near the left field foul line for a game-ending three-run home run. That home run was called the 'Shot Heard 'Round the World.' If you research it you can find a clip of the home run online. The announcer just kept yelling, 'The Giants win the pennant! The Giants win the pennant! The Giants win the pennant! And they're going crazy!' over and over. It was the greatest game I've ever been a part of, even though I was sitting on the bench that day."

The greatest game I've ever been a part of. I never thought I'd hear Grandpa say those words.

"Look here," Grandpa Joe says, smiling. "I have exactly three left—one for each of you."

He places a small cardboard rectangle into each of our hands. It's his official Major League Baseball card.

I see tears well up in Grace's eyes, and I smile wistfully back at her. I know exactly how she feels. We made my grandpa's lifelong dream come true—three kids from Sands Middle School. Who would have ever thought it?

"Okay, so I never set the baseball world on fire," Grandpa Joe admits softly. "But I got to live out my dream, and that's something not many people get to do. Never give up on your dreams, kids. Isn't that what I always tell you, Matty?"

"Always, Grandpa," I reply.

The emotion of the moment is too much for

Grace. She leans over and gives Grandpa Joe one of her special Grace clumsy-but-loving hugs.

"I love you, Grandpa Joe!" she shouts.

Grandpa Joe is surprised, but he hugs her back. Then he laughs.

"You remind me of someone, Gracie," he tells her as he reaches out to smooth her hair.

Then he turns back to us.

"Did I ever tell you about this sweet, kooky girl that had a crush on me? It all started when I wanted to dance with your aunt Patty, Matt. It was at a Fourth of July party at your uncle Alex's house, just before I left for the majors . . ."

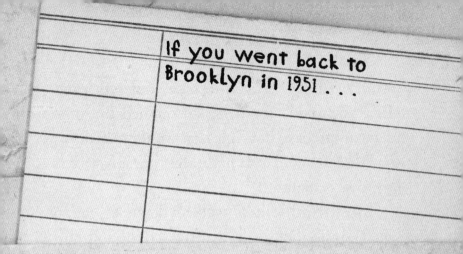

If you went back to Brooklyn in 1951 . . .

Walking the streets of Bay Ridge, Brooklyn, you'd see a lot of the same things that Matt, Grace, and Luis did. The clothes Ms. Tremt picked out for them really did represent the style of the times. (The poodle on the poodle skirt had sparkly rhinestone eyes!)

There was a drive-in fast-food restaurant called Mitchell's on 86th Street and 7th Avenue. If you didn't want to go inside and sit down in a booth to order, you could pull your car into the parking lot and honk the horn to call for a waitress, who would skate over to you to take your order and bring you food. You'd be surrounded by some pretty impressive hot rods that would race down the 7th Avenue strip at night. It's now a Nathan's fast-food restaurant.

The street the kids walked down to get to Uncle Alex's house, 86th Street, was and still is a major shopping area for the neighborhood, although most of the stores have changed. There was an F. W. Woolworth Co. department store with a lunch counter, where you could buy a "super deluxe ham sandwich" for forty cents. Many people called it the "five-and-dime" store because originally most of the items for sale in the store cost a nickel or a dime.

On the way to Uncle Alex's, Matt, Grace, and Luis would have passed a schoolyard where kids would be playing classic Brooklyn games like stickball and skully (or skelly, or skellsies, depending which neighborhood you grew up in). The kids would draw a skully board on the sidewalk with chalk and then flick bottle caps filled with melted wax into numbered squares on the board. They might race to the fire hydrant, which they called a "Johnny pump," or buy a cup of ice cream from the Good Humor man's cart for a dime (and dimes were still made from silver back then).

There is a small, quiet street in Bay Ridge called Harbor View Terrace. The street in the story, Bay Vista Terrace, was based on this real street. Today, if you want to buy a home there, you will need a few million dollars. Backyard swimming pools, though, were a rare thing in the early 1950s in Brooklyn. They started to become popular later in the '50s and '60s, but mostly in the suburbs. Only a few really wealthy people would have had a pool then; most Brooklyn kids went to beaches like Coney Island, or a city pool, to swim.

New York City was the center of the baseball universe in 1951, and the Brooklyn Dodgers were like the sun to most Brooklynites. The team got their name from the "trolley dodgers," and the many trolley lines that once moved people all over the borough. During the 1930s and '40s, the trolleys started being replaced by buses. There were still a few trolleys in 1951, but very few. The ones in Bay Ridge had already stopped running, which is why Matt had to take the subway to Ebbets Field.

There really was a doubleheader between the New York Giants and the Brooklyn Dodgers on July 4, 1951, and Matt would have never gotten in without Uncle Alex's ticket. Fans started lining up outside the stadium the night before. The gates were opened at 8:45 a.m. on July 4, which was a Wednesday that year, and within two hours every seat was sold out. They turned away 15,000 people at the gates that day, and the ballpark was filled to capacity with 34,620 fans.

There really is a drink called an egg cream, and, as Ms. Tremt told the kids, the drink contains neither eggs nor cream! It's a beverage consisting of milk, carbonated water, and chocolate syrup. Nobody knows for sure why it is called an egg cream.

Nat King Cole was one of the most popular singers in the 1950s. He was the first African-American performer to host a weekly TV series, in 1956.

Hilda Chester is one of the most famous fans

in baseball history. Sitting in the bleachers of Ebbets Field, beginning in the 1920s, Chester would yell from the stands at players. Soon reporters were giving her free passes to attend the games, and she was a regular in the outfield. She was also known as the "Queen of the Bleachers" and "Howling Hilda."

Nineteen-year-old Willie Mays really did join the Giants in May 1951. He was on deck when Bobby Thomson hit the "Shot Heard 'Round the World" to win the play-offs against the Brooklyn Dodgers that fall. He left the team for the following two years when he was drafted into the army during the Korean War. When he returned in 1954, he hit 41 home runs and led the league with a .345 batting average. Willie Mays ended up hitting 660 home runs in his career and is in the National Baseball Hall of Fame.

Did you ever wish you were an octopus? I mean, not in the squishy, looking-like-an-undersea-alien kind of way—more like a "you know, having eight arms would be pretty cool right now," feeling. Let me tell you, if I were to see a shooting star, or blow on a dandelion at this very moment, that would be my wish. Jada Reese, girl octopus. I could definitely use at least three more pairs of hands to finish organizing the mess in front of me!

"See you after school?" Abby asks as we pack up our stuff and get ready to head to class.

"Sure, but I have to stop in the library first," I say with a sigh. "Because this."

I hold up my latest spelling test.

Remember how I said I'm not so great with details? Well, I'm more than not so great with spelling details. I'm horrible. Like a fifty-three-on-my-last-spelling-test horrible. I am shockingly bad at spelling. But hey, I'm lucky enough to live in a time when most of my reports can be typed on my laptop and benefit from spell-check. So how important is spelling really when you get into the real world and don't have to take spelling tests anymore?

"Your evil nemesis," Daniel teases as he does a sinister supervillain sneer. "Spellllllling."

Of course Daniel only has to look at a word once and he remembers how to spell it. Again, so not fair.

"It's just one test, Jada," Abby says. "You shouldn't be so hard on yourself."

"I'm not," I say. "But it's not just one test, either. So I will be in the library, hitting the spelling books. Even though spelling is my nemesis."

"Okay," Daniel says. "And by the way, that's not spelled 'O' and 'K.'"

"Got it, wise guy." I laugh.

When the bell for last period rings, I head down the hall to the school library. It's become a pretty popular place since Ms. Tremt took over as the school librarian. She seemed a little strange at first, but once you get to know her, she's really interesting and easy to talk to. She also always weirdly seems to know the exact book you're looking for, which I guess is why a copy of *How to*

Spell Your Way to the T-O-P is sitting on the table as soon as I walk in.

"Wow, thanks, Ms. Tremt," I whisper to myself, not exactly excited about my new reading material. "How did you know?"

I grab the book and sit down at an empty table. I flip through the pages. It's like torture. Here's the thing about spelling. It doesn't make any sense. Take this rule on page forty-three of *How to Spell Your Way to the T-O-P*:

I before *E*, except after *C* . . . or when sounding like "ay" as in "neighbor" or "weigh."

Which makes sense, when you're talking about words like "pie" or "weigh." But then explain to me why W-I-E-R-D is circled in red on my test paper.

But here is the *really* w-e-i-r-d thing. I may have been studying, but I definitely didn't hear a door open, or anyone tiptoe into the room. And even if I hadn't heard Ms. Tremt sneak in, there was no way I could have missed Matt, Grace, and Luis, my friends who just happen to somehow suddenly be standing right behind her.

What's even w-e-i-r-d-e-r is that they look like they've stepped out of the movie *Grease*, all decked out in 1950s-style clothes. The saddle shoes and bobby socks that Grace is wearing haven't been in style since my grandmother was in diapers. And Matt is a jock! He would never slick back his hair and wear cuffed jeans. I don't know if I've ever seen him out of his sweatpants.

"Well done, Grace, Luis, and Matt," Ms. Tremt says, loud enough for everyone in the library to hear. "That is a fabulous magic trick. A very exciting entrance indeed! We'll need to work on it a bit more, but your costumes are perfect for your school project, Fashions Through the Times. Well done!"

The other kids in the library just shake their heads and get back to their books. I can tell they think it's just another wacky Ms. Tremt moment. I disagree. I think it's something bigger than that.

My logical brain is on high alert, so when Ms. Tremt pulls Matt, Grace, and Luis through a door that I never even knew existed before,

I quietly follow them and see that they're in a secret, empty classroom. How is it possible that everyone else in the library missed this?

Matt hands Ms. Tremt a shimmering metallic book. She turns right around and says, "Jada? Here's the book we discussed."

The Book of Memories. Ms. Tremt and I did have a discussion about it, a very intense discussion, a couple of days ago. It happened when I noticed her trying to casually sneak the book into a box. The book is way too glitzy to casually sneak anywhere, though. It shimmers kind of like a '70s disco ball.

Ms. Tremt told me that the book was special in ways that I could never imagine, but that she was holding it for someone else first, and when they were done with it, I was next in line. We talked about how reading a book—especially a great one—was like taking a trip through space and time, but how *this* book would take the reader on a trip in bold, new ways.

Those were exactly her words, by the way— "bold, new ways." It sounded like some sci-fi mumbo jumbo, but it also sounded intriguing and exciting the way Ms. Tremt said it. Like it was a secret she couldn't wait to share with me. And I couldn't wait to dive in to it!

Now that it's here, I can hardly believe I'm holding it in my hands.

I smile at Matt and say, "Did you have a nice trip?" Then I give a little laugh, because I know Ms. Tremt doesn't mean a real trip. She meant reading a good book would take you on a trip in your imagination . . . didn't she?

Matt turns pale and nods silently. He looks like he wants to run away as fast as he can. And that's just what he does. I don't understand his reaction. I mean, who doesn't love a good book, right? I can't wait to start reading this one.

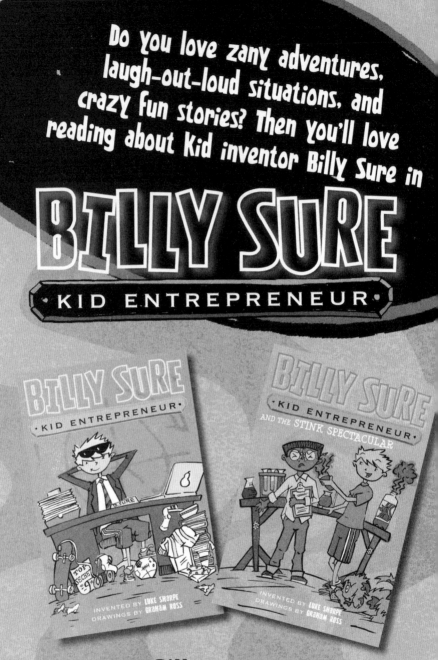